Liberty Divided

by

Alicia Dean

Isle of Fangs Book 2

This is a work of fiction. Names, characters, places, and incidents are either the product of the author's imagination or are used fictitiously, and any resemblance to actual persons living or dead, business establishments, events, or locales, is entirely coincidental.

Liberty Divided

Cover Art by *Lisa Dawn MacDonald*

The Wild Rose Press, Inc.
PO Box 708
Adams Basin, NY 14410-0708
Visit us at www.thewildrosepress.com

Publishing History
First Edition, 2022
Trade Paperback ISBN 978-1-5092-3980-1
Digital ISBN 978-1-5092-3981-8

Previously Self-published
Published in the United States of America

A large bump against her legs made her freeze. That was a big ass fish.

She shuddered and broke the kiss. "What the…?"

"What is it?" Ryan's muscled chest rose and fell with short breaths.

"Some kind of huge…" Liberty looked down, and her heart stuttered to a halt. Trembles shook her body, and a scream tore from her throat.

A woman's pale face stared up at her from just below the surface of the water.

"Bloody hell," Ryan muttered. "Come on."

He took her shoulders and led her onto the sand. Darkness clouded her vision, and the trembles increased.

He tightened his grip. "Look at me, sweetheart." His voice was steady, comforting.

She lifted her eyes.

"Go up the beach and grab your phone. Call 1-7." He gently brushed a strand of damp hair from her face. "Can you do that for me?"

She nodded, still trembling. The second dead girl she'd seen since she arrived—the first one had been at a party Eli had thrown. Even though she'd slain vampires, she wasn't immune to death. Seeing the girls' bodies was far different from hunting vampires. That had been for protection, to prevent evil from taking over the island. This was tragic, heart-breaking.

Ryan gave her a gentle push, and she hurried up the beach, tiny sobs working their way from her chest to her throat.

Fumbling in her bag, she snatched out her cell phone and punched in the digits.

Dedication

To my cousins, Donna Faye Banta Cooper and Debbie Mangrum Wallace, who not-so-patiently awaited the release of this book. (Don't pretend you didn't ambush me at the family reunion). Love you much! And to my cousin, Rebecca Ward, for her unwavering loyalty in reading my books.

Prologue

Sang Croc Island
French Polynesia

The night breeze blowing in from the ocean brought with it the intoxicating aromas of suntan oil and blood. Although there weren't a lot of humans on the beach now that dusk had fallen, the heady scent of the rich, red fluid was strong enough that the vampire could still smell it just beneath the surface of their flesh. He drew in a breath and slowly exhaled. *Delicious*.

The sliver of moon drifted in the black sky and shone on the white sand, providing enough light so that, even if he weren't a vampire, he could still see clearly.

He strolled along the beach, blending in with the handful of human tourists hanging about. He'd been itching for the sun to go down, had barely slept all day. He was hungry. Jonesing for a feed. Mostly, though, he was anxious to put the next phase of his plan in motion. Slow and steady. Wasn't that how the tortoise had won the race?

He strode across the soft sand, looking out at the glassy surface of the ocean—a sight he would never see the way it was meant to be seen, in sunlight. The cruel irony of being a vampire on a tropical island wasn't lost on him.

Ah well, while he was unable to enjoy the daytime,

fortunately, beautiful, tasty women were always out in abundance, even after darkness fell.

Evidence of his prediction came when he spotted two girls in barely-there bikinis at the edge of the ocean. They kicked water on one another, giggling and squealing in oblivious delight.

Girls. They were the easiest.

They passed a bottle of Lambrusco back and forth, chugging straight from the neck. He grinned. How fitting. In a matter of moments, *he* would be chugging straight from the neck.

He approached silently, not speaking until he was within a foot of where they frolicked. "Ladies? Enjoying yourselves?"

They turned startled eyes on him. The expression on the tall brunette's face became a flirty smile. The shorter of the two still looked wary.

"Tons," the brunette said. She held out the bottle. "Want a sip?"

His lips spread into a grin. "More than you can imagine."

She laughed and released the Lambrusco into his grip. He put it to his mouth and drank. The wine was a cheap, sweet red. The taste couldn't compare to the sweet red of the blood flowing through the girls' veins. Veins he would tap into shortly.

"Skyler, we'd better be heading back to the hotel," Miss Blonde, Short, and Skeptical said to her friend.

He moved closer to the blonde and walked into the ocean, ignoring the unpleasant feeling of water-soaked shoes. He stared down, letting his eyes capture hers. "Why is that? The party's only just begun."

She swallowed audibly, and the pulse in her neck

jumped. Excitement bloomed in his chest. He hadn't been sure which one would die, but now he knew. This one had spunk. She would not only taste delicious, conquering her would be more exciting.

She started to look away, but he gripped her chin in his fingers. "What's your name?" he asked softly.

"Mine's Skyler," her friend said from behind him, as if he hadn't just heard the blonde call her by name. "She can go back to the hotel if she wants and—"

"Silence!" He whirled on the brunette. She blinked at him in hurt confusion. Sensitive little thing. For God's sake. It wasn't like he said her bikini made her look fat.

Still holding the blonde's chin, he focused on the brunette's eyes. "Look at me and listen carefully." He kept his voice low, commanding. "Stand there quietly and don't move. Don't make a sound until I tell you it's okay. Understand?"

"Hey," her blonde friend said. "You can't tell her what to do."

He let out a frustrated breath. Mesmerizing two chicks at once was not an easy feat.

He turned back to the blonde and made sure they were eye to eye. Made sure he had her complete attention. "You will also be quiet. Do exactly as I say. Understand?"

A frown marred her brows, but she gave a quick, jerky nod. Barely under. Good. He didn't want her too docile when the time came.

Back to the brunette, he said, "No matter what happens, no matter what you see, you won't make a peep. You won't move. Got it?"

She nodded and immediately quieted. The only sounds were those of crashing waves and distant conversations of other humans.

"Your name?" he demanded again.

"Patrice," she finally muttered.

"Well, Patrice, because you're so enticing, so remarkable, you will have to be sacrificed. But take solace in the fact that your friend will be spared."

She blinked rapidly. Her mouth dropped open, and little mewling sounds came out. "What? I… you're going to…?"

He released her chin and gripped a handful of hair at the back of her head. "Not a sound, I said." She fell silent, and he reveled in the terror-filled eyes. So easy.

He yanked her to him and tugged her head back. With a growl, he protracted his fangs and drove them deep into her flesh.

Hot sweet blood with just a hint of wine flowed into his mouth. He nearly moaned in satisfaction. The feeding was good… great, but being another step closer to exacting revenge… well, that was about as good as it got.

She struggled silently, clawing at his shoulders, trying to shove him away. Nice. He liked a little fight. But the fight soon fled. Her body went limp. The flow of blood slowed. Her heart no longer pumped it to him. He released her, and her body hit the water with a splash.

He turned back to her friend, wiping his mouth with the back of his hand. Silent tears coursed down her cheeks. Her body trembled violently, but she remained silent, standing where he'd left her.

He ignored the flicker of sympathy crowding its way into his soul. He was a vampire, after all. It was in his nature to feed… to kill. No room for a conscience. No room for weakness.

He stalked to the brunette and grabbed her

shoulders, looking down into her eyes. "Listen carefully," he said. "I want you to wait ten minutes, then run up the beach, screaming. Report this to the police. You understand?"

She nodded.

"Good. And this is what you'll tell them…"

Chapter 1

Liberty Van Helsing could almost believe last night had been a dream—that she hadn't hunted vampires, hadn't actually *killed* vampires—had it not been for the aches in every muscle of her body and the bandage on her arm that covered a bullet wound.

Business was slow at the tiki bar. But of course her boss, Jerome, wouldn't let her off early. The Perfect Getaway had to be fully manned at all times, with the bright smiling faces of a staff eager to serve. All she felt like doing was going home and pulling the covers over her head, sleeping for a week.

"How are you making it?" Ryan Kelly spoke at her shoulder as she loaded plates from the warmer onto a tray.

Her pulse quickened at the sound of his voice. She glanced up to find his dark eyes roaming over her from head to toe, worry evident in their black depths. "I'm fine."

He frowned. "I don't think so. Tell me how you're really doing."

She swallowed back a lump of tears. *There's no crying in vampire hunting...*

She'd learned less than a month ago that she was a descendant of the vampire hunter, Van Helsing. She'd traveled from her small Oklahoma hometown to this strange island to meet the father she'd never known existed. And gotten so much more than she bargained for. Her father passed away before she really got to know him. And here she was, destined to take up where he left off. Hunting and slaying vampires when she was barely out of high school, had never even had a fist fight, and the sight of blood made her hurl. Some hunter she was.

"Well, how I'm really doing is, I'm a little freaked about what I did last night." She brushed a hank of hair behind her ear. "My arm hurts like hell, and I've barely slept. Better?"

He shrugged. "More honest, at least." He covered her hand with his. "I'll do whatever I can to help you through this. You know that, right?"

She nodded. "I'll be fine. Really."

He pointed to the tray. "Let me take that. You don't need to be lifting with that arm." He took hold of the tray and scowled at her. "You should have called in."

"I'm fine. I can get this." She tugged on the tray, but he didn't release it. "Ryan, you can't coddle me. And you can't do my job. You're tending bar tonight, and I'll just have to suck it up. Jerome would've had a hissy fit if I'd called in."

"Bloody dingo," he muttered.

Liberty smiled. Although she didn't understand all of his Australian idioms, she was sure the insult fit their boss perfectly. "Come on, get behind the bar, and let me do my job. I appreciate your concern, but if I'm going to be a hunter, I need to suck it up, get tougher."

He winked and flashed his adorable grin, making the laugh lines around his eyes more pronounced. "I like you soft, just like you are."

Warmth spread through her belly, and she smiled self-consciously. "Thanks."

She liked Ryan. Maybe not as much as he liked her, but he was ten times better than the cheating boyfriend she'd left behind in Oklahoma.

She lifted the tray and instantly regretted not taking Ryan up on his offer. Her wound screamed with the weight, even though she was using her good arm to bear most of it.

Gritting her teeth against the pain, she headed to the table. Female laughter shrieked through the room, and Liberty knew exactly where it came from.

She smiled at her customers, but inside she seethed. Eli was here with two girls. How dare he show his face after what had happened last night? It wasn't like the Getaway was the only bar on the island.

"Jerk," she mumbled under her breath. "Can I get you anything else?" she asked the two couples she was serving.

"We'll have another round."

"Coming right up." She put the empty tray on the rack and started toward the bar to order the drinks, glancing at her other tables to make sure they didn't need anything, and tried to ignore Eli Barkley.

But in spite of her determination, her eyes strayed to his table. He was leaned back in his seat, arms draped on the backs of the bamboo chairs on either side of him. Each chair held a female—one blonde and one with flaming red hair—both with envy-inducing curves.

Eli's dark blond hair was in its usual disarray, his silver eyes glinting as he laughed. His pose was relaxed, like nothing had happened. Like she wasn't in the room. Like he didn't give a damn.

Fine. She didn't give a damn either.

Lips compressed, she stalked to the bar. "Two

margaritas, a hurricane, and a Bloody Mary."

Ryan peered at her, eyes narrowed. "You okay?"

She nodded. "Yeah, I'm okay. It's just that Eli is getting under my skin."

"Did he say something to you?"

"No," she admitted reluctantly. "I just think he could have picked a different place to drink and whore around after what happened last night."

"You know, it's really not his fault. It was kind of a dick move for me to tell you he used to be one of the Evil Ones."

Both good and bad vampires inhabited the island. The EO's not only fed, but drained the life from some of their victims—and they turned as many humans as they could each full moon night, which was the only night a human could be turned. Her job was to hunt them and prevent them from multiplying so the island wouldn't be overrun with their kind.

She compressed her lips. "No, it was a dick move that you didn't tell me in the beginning. I had a right to know who would be training me. Who I'd be spending hours alone with."

"Yeah, but he's different now. He's on our side."

Her gaze went back to the table. Irritation tightened her voice. "I think Eli is only on *Eli's* side."

Ryan slid the drinks onto her tray. "He's not a bad sort, really."

The friendship between Ryan and Eli baffled her. A thoughtful, sensitive human and a lying, heartless, jerkwad vampire. *Go figure.* She stole another glance at Eli and his companions. "Who are those girls?"

"I don't know the blonde, but the redhead is Grace. She's a… friend… from Eli's past. They met during the

Civil War."

The Civil War? Even though she knew of the existence of vampires, she couldn't help but be stunned at the reality of it all.

"How old is Eli?" She'd never asked the question. It hadn't really occurred to her that he could possibly be centuries old.

"Twenty-one in human years. In vampire years, he's about two-hundred and fifty. He was turned in the 1700's."

She shook her head. Unbelievable. He'd been around in the Revolutionary War. It seemed implausible, but she knew it was true. The last month had taught her that nothing was beyond the realm of possibility.

"I know." Ryan grinned. "Hard to accept, right? It took me a while. I would say you'll get used to it, but I still haven't."

"I totally get that." She took the tray of drinks to her table and dropped the check. "I'll take care of that whenever you're ready." Maybe they would get the hint. It was closing time, and there were only a few customers left, Eli and his friends included. At least they weren't in her section. She could go as soon as her last table left.

"Here, we'll take care of it now." One of the men offered her a credit card.

Relieved, she accepted the card. She could finish up her closing duties and take off. Finally.

After clearing her section and settling her money for the evening, she headed to the parking lot.

Her first several weeks on the island, she'd had to depend on rides from others. But Antoine—the manservant she'd inherited from her dead father—had insisted she have her own transportation, and they'd purchased a nearly-new blue Corolla for her use. She was still nervous driving in a strange country, but it was damn convenient to have her own wheels.

The Perfect Getaway sat on the beach, and the parking lot was lined with palm trees and red and pink hibiscus plants. The scent of vanilla orchids hung in the air. Such a paradise, yet it held such darkness and evil. She shivered.

"Rough night?"

She jumped at the sound of Eli's voice. *Speaking of darkness and evil…*

She turned a glare on him. He stood directly behind her, hands shoved in his pockets, yet he'd been in the bar only seconds ago.

"Don't do that," she snapped. She looked back at the tiki bar. "How the hell did you…?" She shook her head. "Never mind. You're a vampire. You move with the speed of light."

He grinned and slanted his upper body toward her. "Yeah, but we've got all that darkness brewing inside. Ironic, isn't it?"

She swung away from him and took hold of the door handle. "Whatever. I'm tired, so you'll understand if I don't feel like hanging out and bantering with you. Besides, your dates are waiting for you."

"Jealous?"

She snorted a laugh. "No. Sympathetic. Better them than me."

"Why is it I don't believe you?"

"Maybe because you're delusional?" She gave him an overly sweet smile before turning away to jerk the car door open.

"I see you're still pouting because I didn't tell you I

was once a big, bad vampire."

"It doesn't matter. You warned me early on not to trust you. I should have listened."

"And now you should put on your big girl panties and get over it. You're a hunter, Liberty. You need to toughen up."

Toughen up? Was he kidding? She'd risked her life last night, had worked her ass off training, and he was calling her a wimp. To hell with him. She started to slide into the car, but his voice stopped her.

"You can be mad at me all you want, but you can't completely shut me out."

"Watch me," she bit out, not turning around.

"Let me ask you something. What difference would it have made if you'd known in the beginning?"

She slammed the door and whirled on him. "At least I'd have known who—*what*—I was dealing with."

"Would you still have let me train you?"

"I'm not sure. But I had the right to know. To have all the facts before making that decision."

"If you had chosen not to let me train you, how do you think you would have fared last night? Not knowing the truth was for your own good."

She gave a bitter laugh. "Yeah, and I'm sure you're all about what's best for me."

"Look, you're going to have to put all that behind you. Like it or not, you still need me."

"No, I don't. I'll keep practicing. I'll be fine."

"You can't take that chance. If I hadn't saved your ass last night, we wouldn't be having this conversation."

Just like him to throw *that* in her face. She huffed out a sigh of irritation. "Thanks, but from here on out, I can take care of myself."

He stepped closer, backing her up to the door. The only way she could get away from him was to climb inside the car. But she didn't.

"What's wrong?" He raised his eyebrows, amusement lifting the corners of his mouth. "Are you afraid of me now?"

She tilted her chin up and met his eyes. Eyes that were molten grey in the semi-darkness. "Not afraid. Pissed off. There's a difference."

He chuckled. "Well, it's nice to know I have an effect on you." His gaze dropped to her throat. "Your pulse is beating like crazy. Right here." He stroked a finger down her neck, sending heat skittering over her flesh. *Damn him.* She sucked in a breath and clenched her teeth.

"I can see it." He dropped his hand, and his gaze locked onto hers. "No matter how much you'd like to be, you're not immune to me, Liberty Van Helsing."

She swallowed hard, trying to slow her racing pulse. "I need to get home. Let me go."

His lips curved in a grin, and his voice lowered to a near whisper. "I'm not touching you."

Chapter 2

Eli stepped out into the balmy darkness with his two companions. They'd closed down the tiki bar and had to vacate. Besides, it lost some of its appeal once Liberty left. Tormenting her was so much fun. She was so quick to rise to the bait. Her moss green eyes would darken, and her full lips would tighten. Her chest would rise and fall with angry breaths…

He inwardly groaned. Yeah, *fun to torment*. That's why he screwed with her. It had nothing to do with his wanting a reaction from her, any kind of reaction as long as her focus was on him. Pathetic. What kind of self-respecting bad ass vampire would let a slip of a girl like her consume his thoughts?

But like it or not, she had. Now he'd pissed her off and she might not agree to let him continue to train her. If she didn't, she would die. It was that simple. There was no way she had acquired the skills she needed to be a true Van Helsing. Now that the Evil Ones knew of her existence, she had more to worry about than the feeding frenzy during full moons. She'd have to watch her back nightly. Not to mention, the EOs' big bad leader, Rupert, was now focused on her and would stop at nothing to make her his. She definitely needed Eli's help, but she was too damn stubborn to accept it.

"You're not thinking of that little Van Helsing girl, are you?" Grace's whisper penetrated his reverie. "She's cute, Eli, but looks to be way more trouble than she's worth." Her eyes raked the blonde walking in front of them. "Besides, we have something much more pressing at the moment." She winked. "Dinner."

Eli chuckled. "You always did have a thing for blondes."

She shrugged. "They taste... sweeter somehow."

He and Grace had met in 1863. He'd joined the Union out of boredom and met her when the savage group of soldiers he'd aligned himself with had raided her Georgia plantation. They'd slain her servants and her husband, then decided to have a little fun with Grace before killing her too.

Although having a conscience was not usually his forte, something about her quiet terror, the attempt at courage reflected in her dark brown eyes, her soft flesh... the blue vein visible along the side of her pale neck, he'd had a change of heart. He'd turned on his men. In a matter of seconds, he slaughtered all five of them. Grace had been more terrified than grateful.

"What kind of monster are you?" she'd stammered, her voice rising with panic.

"The kind that saved your ass." He'd jerked her to her feet, stared into her eyes, and mesmerized her into being compliant.

He had to wait for a full moon before he could turn her. That was five days away. During that time, they remained at her plantation. He fed on her, had sex with her—after a few days, she'd initiated it, he hadn't had to mesmerize her for that. Then on the full moon, he'd turned her. They'd been close friends and occasional sexual partners since then. Once in a while, she popped in to hang out and party with him.

As was the way in the vampire procreation process, since he'd turned her, she'd taken on his characteristics and had been as cold-hearted and bloodthirsty as he when he'd been one of the Evil Ones. Once he switched sides, he'd convinced her to subdue her murderous instincts. With a lot of coaxing and a bit of commanding, she'd come around to his way of thinking. But, like him, she had to constantly fight her dark urges.

"We're not going to kill her," he told her now.

She pouted but gave a brief nod. "I know that. I'll control myself, I promise."

They'd been walking along the beach and had reached the edge of the water. The blonde stopped and turned to face them. She was in her late thirties with the worn, desperate look of someone who'd partied too much too soon and was heading toward burnout.

"So?" She lifted a brow. "Are we going to do something insanely risky or not?"

Grace's husky laughter filled the night. "Oh my dear, you have no idea how insane… or how risky."

****

Liberty nestled deeper into the beach towel lying on the soft white sand. A cool breeze drifted over her exposed flesh, even though the warmth of the sun beamed down. Ryan's strong hands rubbed sunscreen onto her back and shoulders.

Heaven.

She almost didn't think about the insanity her life had become. Or her run-in with Eli the night before. Or the fact that she missed home, missed her mom so much it was a physical ache. She would call her mother when she got back to the house. But right now, she just wanted to bask in mindless bliss…

"Liberty?" Ryan's hands slowed.

"Hmmm?" she murmured, not opening her eyes. Why did he have to spoil the moment with talking?

"Are you going to let Eli continue training you?"

She let out a heavy sigh. Especially talking about *that*.

She rose and reluctantly dislodged Ryan's skilled hands. "No. I don't trust him."

Ryan sat back on his haunches and beseeched her with his dark brown eyes. "If you don't, you could get hurt. Or worse. And it would be my fault."

She stood and brushed sand off her black two piece. "How would it be your fault?"

Ryan rose to his feet. "Because I told you the truth about him. If I hadn't, you'd still let him train you."

"Ugh. Do we have to talk about Eli on such a beautiful day?"

"Not if you at least promise me you'll consider it."

She hesitated then, realizing it wasn't a commitment, said, "I'll consider it."

He smiled, his white teeth flashing against his bronze skin. "That's all I ask." He took her hand. "Now, come with me."

He tugged lightly, and she followed him down the beach until they were knee-deep in the warm, translucent blue-green water.

"Look."

She followed Ryan's gaze, and let out a gasp. She could see all the way to the ocean floor. What appeared to be hundreds of tiny fish—ranging in hues from jade to orange to one that was the color of a rainbow—swarmed around a purplish cactus-like mound.

"Is that coral?" she asked.

"It is. *Pocillopora*, one of the hundreds of species found in the Pacific."

"My God," she whispered in awe. "It's unbelievable."

"So are you." Ryan took her hands and tugged her to him. Their bodies lightly bumped, his warm and hard and damp, hers wanting to melt into him.

He caressed her knuckles with his thumbs. "I'm bloody bonkers over you, you know that right?"

She nodded. "I like you too, Ryan. A lot." The way her pulse rate accelerated and goose bumps pebbled her flesh, she was feeling more than just 'like,' but she wasn't ready to go there. Not yet.

"I know you have feelings for Eli, too."

Eli again. She opened her mouth to protest, but he placed a finger over her lips. "You hate him right now, because he hurt you. But I've seen the way you look at him. The way he looks at you. I know there's something there, and it's okay. Because I'm a very patient bloke. You mean too much to me to give up so soon."

She smiled. "We've known each other barely a month."

"I know. That's what makes it so bloody great, right? That we could be this in sync this soon." He slipped his hands around her waist, pulled her closer.

Her breathing slowed, her heart thumping so loudly she was sure he must have heard it. Her lips tingled in anticipation of his kiss.

"Yeah." Her voice cracked. "Bloody great."

He smiled. "You're gorgeous, love. The golden highlights in your chestnut hair shimmer in the sunlight. Your green eyes look like emeralds… a beautiful day with a beautiful girl. It doesn't get any better." His voice lowered. "You know, this is something you could never share with Eli."

A pang of sympathy pierced her heart. What must it be like to live for centuries in the dark? To never feel heavenly sunlight on your face?

She frowned. "Is this your way of one-upping him?"

Ryan grinned. "I guess so. Sorry. Not exactly the way to be the better man, is it?"

She laughed and ran a hand over the *carpe diem* tattoo in his right bicep. "It's not a competition. If it were, you'd be in the lead."

His eyes roamed her face and settled on her lips. He cupped a hand behind her head, his fingers firm on her scalp, the other hand pressing into the small of her back. He bent his head, touched his lips to hers, and all thoughts of Eli fled.

While they kissed, small fish bumped against her legs—which felt a little creepy and cool at the same time. Ryan's lips on hers, the deep growl in his throat fusing with the sighs coming from hers, was so different, so... magical. A few months ago, she never could have imagined she'd be standing in the South Pacific kissing a gorgeous guy. Of course, she never imagined she'd be out of Oklahoma. Let alone a world away.

She lifted on her tip toes, parted her lips, and Ryan's tongue slipped inside. Her knees nearly buckled as she was swept away in a torrent of desire she'd never felt before—most definitely not with Cam. On one hand, she hated PDA, knew she should pull away. On the other, this was the most amazing, scariest, and at the same time perfect thing she'd ever experienced, and she didn't want it to stop.

Somewhere in the back of her mind she wondered...

if they were alone, exactly how would this end? Would she give up her virginity to him? The way she felt at this moment, she would be powerless to resist.

A large bump against her legs made her freeze. *That* was a big ass fish.

She shuddered and broke the kiss. "What the…?"

"What is it?" Ryan's muscled chest rose and fell with short breaths.

"Some kind of huge…" Liberty looked down, and her heart stuttered to a halt. Trembles shook her body, and a scream tore from her throat.

A woman's pale face stared up at her from just below the surface of the water.

"Bloody hell," Ryan muttered. "Come on."

He took her shoulders and led her onto the sand. Darkness clouded her vision, and the trembles increased.

He tightened his grip. "Look at me, sweetheart." His voice was steady, comforting.

She lifted her eyes.

"Go up the beach and grab your phone. Call 1-7." He gently brushed a strand of damp hair from her face. "Can you do that for me?"

She nodded, still trembling. The second dead girl she'd seen since she arrived—the first one had been at a party Eli had thrown. Even though she'd slain vampires, she wasn't immune to death. Seeing the girls' bodies was far different from hunting vampires. That had been for protection, to prevent evil from taking over the island. This was tragic, heart-breaking.

Ryan gave her a gentle push, and she hurried up the beach, tiny sobs working their way from her chest to her throat.

Fumbling in her bag, she snatched out her cell phone

and punched in the digits.

While she listened to the rings, she watched Ryan. He shouted at the swimmers, waving his arms and motioning for them to come out of the water. Then he bent and gently pulled the girl's body onto the shore. Maybe it was a bad idea to touch her, tainting evidence and all, but if he didn't, she could possibly float away and they'd never find her. She'd no doubt be devoured by scavengers…

Bile rose to Liberty's throat, and she squeezed her eyes shut to banish the image.

"One-seven, what is your emergency?" A French-accented female voice came on the line.

Liberty's teeth chattered, even though warmth still blazed down from the sun. "There's been a…" she was going to say murder, but they didn't know how the girl had died. "…death. We found a girl. Her body. She's…"

"Are you positive that she is deceased?"

The bloated, pale face rose to her mind. "I'm sure," Liberty choked out.

"Okay. Please provide your location, and do not touch the body."

Uh, yeah, no worries. At least not again. Been there, done that.

Liberty spoke quickly, providing the necessary details.

After ending the call, she forced her feet to carry her back down the beach to the edge of the water, where Ryan, head bowed, knelt next to the dead girl like a dejected sentinel.

****

Later that evening, Liberty stood at the door of the police station, holding the coin Ryan had given her and rubbing her thumb along the impressions, trying to calm her nerves. She took a deep breath, and pushed the glass door open.

She'd never been in a police station before. What did they want with her? She'd answered their questions at the beach. When the call came from the captain asking her to meet him at the station, she hadn't known what to make of it. Ryan offered to come with her, but she couldn't lean on him for everything. As Eli so ingeniously put it, she needed to put on her big girl panties.

Ugh. Why did she always have to think about Eli? He was *such* a pain… she shouldn't give him a second thought.

"Liberty?" A woman stood next to a receptionist desk. Behind her, more glass doors led into a squad room. "I am Aiata. You may come on back." She was in her late twenties, pretty, a native judging from the caramel skin and dark, exotic eyes. A long black braid fell down the middle of her back.

Liberty followed her past two desks overflowing with stacks of papers, one empty, the other occupied by a middle-aged man in a uniform.

Aiata stopped at the back of the squad room, in front of a door with a sign reading "Captain Jacquard." The office windows were glass, but shades covered them so Liberty couldn't see inside. Aiata opened the door. "Here she is, gentlemen."

Liberty stepped inside the room and her throat knotted with anxiety. A large-chested man stood from his seat behind a desk and extended his hand. "Liberty, I'm Captain Jacquard. I think you know these gentlemen."

Rupert Kilbourne lounged in a chair across from the captain's desk. Next to him sat a guy she didn't recognize. He was a few years older than she was, fit, dark-haired, attractive.

He smiled and winked. "So you must be the infamous Liberty Van Helsing. Finally, we meet." He offered his hand, and she shook it. "You don't know me. I'm Blake, Rupert's son."

Oh God, there was an offspring?

Rupert came to his feet and took her hand, bowing. He placed a lingering kiss on the back. "Liberty, my dear, lovely to see you again." His silver hair and blue eyes gave him a distinguished, handsome appearance, but a glint of evil hovered somewhere amidst all that charm.

She jerked her hand back and resisted the urge to wipe away his touch. Her gaze went to the final occupant of the room. He stood, gave a small mock bow and a crooked grin. "Yes, Liberty, *lovely* to see you again."

Eli.

Chapter 3

Liberty looked at the captain. "What are they doing here? In fact, what am *I* doing here?"

"Please, sit." In spite of his size, the captain's voice was smooth, reassuring. "I will explain everything. I appreciate your coming to meet with us."

"I didn't realize they would be here, or I would have declined the offer."

A hard gleam came into his brown eyes. "Then I would have had to come to you. This is a matter of utmost importance, I assure you. Please hear me out."

Liberty tightened her lips and dropped into a chair flanked by Rupert and Eli. She felt like a gazelle caught between a lion and a cheetah.

Eli leaned over and whispered, "Where's your shadow?"

The touch of his breath against her ear sent a shiver coursing through her. She shifted away and ignored his question.

"First off," Captain Jacquard said. "I wanted to tell you how very sorry I am about the incident this afternoon. That must have been quite traumatizing."

"It was… difficult… yes."

"I am afraid to inform you that this young lady was not the first victim of a similar attack."

Liberty snorted a sarcastic laugh. "You mean a vampire attack?" She shot a glance at Rupert, then at Eli.

24

"I must say that doesn't come as a surprise, Captain. There is no shortage of vicious vampires on the island."

Rupert spoke from her left. "But these are different. Even the vampires of my… *persuasions*… have certain guidelines they must follow. We try to be—discreet— when choosing our sustenance. Although at times, our nature takes over and, how shall I put this, our *vessels* do not survive, we certainly do not condone frequent, public slaughter."

She raised her brows and forced a note of mock admiration into her voice. "My, you guys are regular altar boys."

A deep chuckle rumbled from his chest. "You are a little spitfire, are you not?" He looked past her to Eli. "You shall have your hands full with this one, my boy."

Liberty scowled. "*He'll* have his hands full? I can't imagine why. My plan is to avoid him as much as possible."

"That is what I wanted to speak with you about," the captain interjected. He was silent for several moments, his bushy brows lowered into a scowl. "You and Eli are going to have to work together to stop whoever is committing these crimes."

Shock rendered her speechless. When she found her voice, she said, "Work with *him*? No way." She shook her head vehemently. "No freakin' way."

"Yes, Captain," Eli said. "I'm afraid Liberty, in spite of her Van Helsing heritage, is a bit of a weakling. She learned one tiny little thing about me, and now she acts like I'm the anti-Christ. In spite of the fact that more innocent victims will die if we don't stop this person, we need to consider Miss Van Helsing's fragile emotional state. I'm afraid it will be more than she can handle to work with the likes of me."

With each word he spoke, fury built inside Liberty's chest. She pushed to her feet and whirled on him. "How dare you! Just because I don't trust you, don't want to be within twenty feet of you, doesn't mean I'm a weakling, or fragile. You have a lot of fu—" She halted and took a deep breath. "A lot of freakin' nerve talking that way about me." She didn't know who she was more furious with, Eli, or herself for confirming his assessment and acting like a weakling. She swallowed and continued, "I am not afraid of you. And of course I don't want more innocent people to die. I'll hear the captain out, but I would appreciate it if you would stop… baiting me."

He smiled. "But you rise to the bait so easily. I find it… irresistible."

The way he said 'irresistible' indicated more than just *baiting* her. A shiver ran down her spine that wasn't completely unpleasant.

Liberty forced her thoughts away from Eli and sat, directing her attention to the captain. "Of course I will do whatever I can." She wrinkled her nose in distaste at Eli. "And work with whoever—*whatever*—I have to in order to stop this person. I'm not sure what I can do that the police can't, though. What either of us can do."

Captain Jacquard tapped his fingers on the desktop and frowned. "First of all, the laws on the island are… different. Vampire crimes are to be handled by Van Helsings. After your father's death, we thought they would fall under our jurisdiction." His gaze rose and he leveled her a look that was less than friendly. "Now that you're here, vampire crimes fall to you. I suppose it makes sense. With your hunter skills, and with Eli having been on both sides of the fence, so to speak, the two of you should make a good team. Eli can garner insight into this person's thinking, his—or her—habits, that we cannot." The captain's features sagged, as if he'd aged in front of her eyes. "Additionally, once we find this person, arresting him will be futile. All he has to do is morph into a bat and escape. Or mesmerize our jailers. All manner of options are open to vampires. Which means a different kind of justice is needed to stop this rogue." He pursed his mouth and his frowned deepened. "We'd hoped to contain this, but these latest murders have drawn media attention. Tourism could suffer. The peace of mind of our residents and tourists will be shattered if we do not put an end to it."

"I see." And she did see, but she didn't have to like the fact that she'd be working with Eli. A hunter teaming up with a vampire? Ridiculous.

"And of course," the captain said. "My people will offer our assistance in identifying this maniac, but the rest is up to you and Eli."

Liberty looked at Rupert. "How does this involve you and your son?"

The captain answered for him. "Rupert and Blake want to help because this rogue is endangering their food source and will keep tourists from visiting our island. When your father was alive, the island was in good hands." His gaze flicked to Rupert. "He kept the population of—dangerous vampires to a minimum. Now, they have multiplied. And as I am sure you are aware, when a vampire sires someone, that new vampire takes on his or her inclinations. Sometimes, they are able to overcome their more—vicious traits, but it is rare. That is another area of grave importance in utilizing your assistance. If you are able to stop this person, their entire line will cease procreating. It will halt any offshoot of evil that might otherwise develop."

As much as Liberty hated to admit it, the captain made sense. It was settled. She would be working with Eli. What would Ryan think about that? It wasn't like Ryan owned her, but she cared about him and didn't want him to worry about her and Eli spending time together. She would just have to make sure Ryan understood that she had no interest in Eli whatsoever. "What's our first step?"

The captain picked up a baggie from his desk and handed it to her. Inside was a small wrinkled sheet of paper. Liberty smoothed it out through the plastic and looked up with a frown. "I don't understand. It's a drawing of a tree."

"That's really all we have, other than our eye witness. It was crumpled in her hand. She said the killer gave it to her."

"What does it mean?"

"We don't know. Yet. I wanted you to see it in case something similar comes up in your inquiry." He reached for the bag, and she handed it back. "We need to go over your statement from this afternoon."

"I already told the officer who came out what happened."

"Yes, I know. But sometimes after a few hours, new details emerge. So, if you will bear with me, we will quickly run through the events leading up to your discovery of the body."

"Yes. Sure."

"Okay. You and Ryan Kelly were standing in the water. The girl's body bumped against your leg, is that correct?"

Revulsion at the memory washed over her, and she shuddered. "That's correct."

"What were you doing that you did not see the body before that time?"

She lifted her brows, surprised at the directness of the question. "What was I—doing?"

"Yes. You and Ryan were in the water, but I assume you were facing away from the location of the body. What were you doing that kept you from noticing the body before?"

Her insides went cold. She felt Eli's eyes on her, felt him waiting. She took a deep breath and swallowed hard. "I—we—were... kissing."

She glanced at Eli from the corners of her eyes. Other than a brow lifted in amusement, there was no reaction from him.

"You and Kelly?" This from Blake. "Well, well, the bloke works fast." He grinned at Eli. "He scooped the pretty girl up right from under your nose, eh?"

Eli frowned, but didn't respond.

The captain cleared his throat. "If we can get on with this, please?" He said to Liberty, "What happened next?"

She repeated her story, just as she had to the first responder on the scene. She ended with the part about Ryan kneeling next to the dead girl. About his keeping people away and protecting the girl's dignity.

"So heroic," Eli murmured.

Liberty shot him a glare.

"Is there anything else you can think of?" Captain Jacquard asked. "Anyone around who seemed suspicious, out of place? Sinister?"

"No, Captain. I believe all of those—" She paused, deliberately turning to Rupert, then to Eli. "—*types* were sleeping at the time."

Rupert burst into laughter. She kept her eyes on the captain.

"Okay, I guess that's all there is to do here. I need you and Eli to take care of something before you go. We have the friend of the victim here at the station. She was with the girl when the attack happened. I asked her to come in. I thought the two of you could speak with her. Liberty, you can perhaps put her at ease and get more details from her, being a young woman about her age. And as for Eli...." He scowled down at his desk then raised his gaze. "Eli, I was hoping you could... mesmerize her. Make her forget she witnessed her friend's death."

"What?" Liberty couldn't control her surprise. "You want a witness to forget the details of a murder?"

"Once we get all the information we need, yes." The captain's tone was defensive. "Remembering will not do us any good, nor will it benefit her. The media is already having a field day with this thing. I don't want them talking to her, blowing her story out of proportion, sensationalizing the whole mess."

In spite of the overlying ridiculousness of the situation, Liberty understood where the captain was coming from.

"So, if that is all then." Rupert stood and took both of Liberty's hands in his, pulling her to her feet. Without even thinking, she allowed it. Her brain was too overwhelmed with all she'd learned to be concerned about his touching her. "I believe the two of you will make a great team." He looked over her shoulder at Eli. "The four of us actually." A crooked smile lifted his mouth. "Shall we call it an unholy alliance?"

****

Skyler Simmons was waiting for them in a bleak interrogation room with gray walls and a lone table. She looked up when they walked in. Her face was damp, streaked with mascara. She twisted her hands nervously together atop the table.

Liberty sat across from the girl and introduced herself and Eli. Eli took the chair next to Skyler.

"I'm so, so sorry about what happened to your friend, to Patrice," Liberty said gently. "I can't imagine how awful that must have been for you."

Skyler nodded and wiped her face, smearing the black beneath her eyes. "I—I can't believe it. I still just can't…" Shaking her head, she dropped her head to stare at her clasped hands. Her shoulders shook.

"Can you tell us about that night? I know it's difficult, but we want to find the man who hurt Patrice, and we need your help."

She drew in a shuddering breath. "Patrice and I were just hanging out. We were drinking a little, you know, laughing, having a good time. Then this guy comes up, this attractive guy…" Her gaze went to Eli and she squinted. "He actually looked a lot like you."

Eli gifted her with a dazzling smile. "Oh, come now, I'm blushing."

Liberty rolled her eyes. "You say he looked a 'lot' like Eli. Can you be more specific? Describe him to me."

Skyler leaned her head back and stared up at the ceiling. "He was tall, but not mega tall, not like a basketball player or anything. He had sort of dark blond hair and light grey eyes…" Her voice trailed off and she looked at Eli once more. "A *lot* like you."

A chill ran over Liberty's arms. It couldn't have

been Eli, could it? No. No way. He wouldn't be sitting there playing Mr. Calm and Cool if it were him. Besides, the girl would just say it was him instead of that it *looked* like him. There had to be more vampires around with that mussed blond hair and those silver eyes…

Liberty took a breath, cleared her throat. "I know this is difficult, Skyler, but can you tell me what he said when he approached? Exactly what happened?"

Hesitantly, tearfully, the girl told her story. "He—he bit her. Oh my God, he tore into her neck, drained her blood, while I just stood there… and… watched." Her body shook and she turned stricken eyes to Liberty. "I know it seems impossible, but I also know what I saw. A vampire murdered Patrice." A sob tore from her throat. "Vampires… oh my God. How can that be?" The words ended in a scream.

Liberty rushed around the table and bent to wrap her arms around Skyler. "I'm so sorry. I know what it's like to lose a best friend." *But not in such a horrifying way as this.* No, she knew what it was like to find out your best friend, someone you'd known most of your life, was a cheating backstabber.

Liberty pulled away and plucked a tissue from the box on the table, handing it to Skyler. "Okay, now I want you to sit very still and listen to my friend here. He has something he wants to tell you."

Liberty stepped back, leaned against the wall, crossed her arms, and watched.

Eli covered the girl's hands with his. In a low, soft, voice he said, "Skyler, I want you to look into my eyes. Listen to me carefully, okay? Can you do that for me?"

Hesitantly, she nodded, her gaze fixed on him.

"There's a good girl. I know what you saw was

horrible. I know you must have been terrified. I'm going to help you with that. I'm going to take the bad memories, the fear, away. You never saw the man who did this to Patrice, okay? The two of you were hanging out, having a good time, drinking… then you decided to go up the beach to talk to some people. Patrice wanted to stay. After a few minutes, you heard sirens. They told you that Patrice had died, but you didn't see anything. You didn't witness her death."

Eli gave the girl a tender, reassuring smile—one Liberty had never seen him use on her. Maybe he was capable of *some* decency.

They left the girl in Aiata's care and walked out into the night. The moisture had become a light misting rain. The island was a quiet, wet, dark oasis.

"Well, we didn't learn anything helpful," Eli said. "All we know is that our killer is a devastatingly, handsome, sexy guy."

"Good Lord." Liberty huffed out a sigh. "And that he's full of himself and exaggerates his attributes."

Eli lifted his hands as if in surrender. "Hey, those were her words, not mine."

"Uhm, actually they were *your* words. All she said was that he was attractive, and that he looked like you."

He shrugged and winked. "That's all I said too."

Liberty nearly growled in irritation. Working with him was going to be pure torture.

Chapter 4

"So, are you going to the festival Tuesday night?" Bianca, Ryan's sister, hopped on a barstool next to where Liberty stood, waiting for customers. Business had been slow all day, and she was bored senseless.

"I'm not sure."

Bianca cast a glance at Ryan, who was stocking bottles on the shelves behind the bar. "My brother asked you, didn't he?"

"Yes, but I might be working."

"You're not scheduled."

Liberty cringed at her slip. She'd meant working with Eli, but that wasn't something she wanted spread around the Getaway. "Right, but I offered to come in if Jerome needed me."

The front door opened and Grace, Eli's vampire friend, walked in—more like glided in. She was a beautiful woman, and she moved with catlike grace. She had vibrant red hair, sapphire blue eyes, flawless skin. and full, red lips. Her body made Liberty's look like that of a school boy.

Grace took a seat in Liberty's section, and Liberty reluctantly headed to her table. She considered asking Bianca to serve Grace, but that wouldn't be in keeping with her bad ass hunter persona.

"What can I get you?" Liberty asked, plastering on a professional smile and playing it off like she didn't recognize her.

Grace's lips stretched into a lazy grin and her eyes dropped to Liberty's neck. "Well, sugah," she drawled. "If I didn't know you were a Van Helsing, I'd sip from that lovely neck of yours. Instead, I'll have a White Russian."

The feral gleam in Grace's eyes made Liberty's insides tense. "Coming right up."

She gave the drink order to Ryan, wishing this wasn't a slow time and Grace wasn't her only customer. Ryan set the cocktail on her tray and narrowed his eyes. "Are you okay?"

"Of course. She doesn't scare me."

"I meant after yesterday. After your visit with the captain."

She shrugged. "I'm not thrilled about what he asked me to do, but I know it's important. I can't stand the thought of some murdering vamp out there preying on innocent people."

He gently stroked her cheek. "That's my girl."

His words and the look in his eyes sent a tremor through her body. She was really falling for this guy. No one had ever cared about her the way he did, had ever looked at her like she was some kind of precious gift. She smiled, he winked, and she melted just a little more.

On shaky legs, she took Grace her drink.

"Anything else?" Liberty asked.

"As a matter of fact, there is. Why don't you sit down and have a chat?"

"I'm sorry. I'm working."

"Oh, now, come on. You're not busy. I'm sure your boss wouldn't mind if you took a teensy weensy break."

How had Grace not lost the southern accent after

traveling the world for a hundred and fifty years? Maybe it was a put on. Whatever it was, it made Liberty's skin crawl. She didn't trust this woman. Didn't want to 'chat' with her for even five seconds.

"No, really. He's pretty strict about stuff like that."

"Jerome!" Grace kept her eyes on Liberty as she shouted for the manager of the bar.

In no time, Jerome was at the table. "Yes? What can I do for you?"

Grace looked up at him, captured his eyes with hers. *Unfreakin' believable.* She was going to mesmerize him?

"Listen to me carefully." Grace's sultry voice lost its accent.

Jerome nodded.

"Your little waitress here, Liberty, is going to sit down and take a break. She's going to visit with me for a bit, and you're going to allow it. You won't only allow it, you're going to be ecstatically grateful that she's doing it."

Jerome nodded again.

Grace smiled like a satisfied lioness. "Now be a good boy and get the girl a drink." She turned back to Liberty. "There. All settled. What would you like?"

Liberty considered still refusing, but she wasn't sure what the consequence would be. Grace might mesmerize Jerome into stripping off his clothes or something. And no one wanted to see that.

She let out a sigh and dropped into the chair across from Grace. "Tropical tea."

Jerome nodded vigorously. "Coming right up. Thank you, Liberty."

Oh geez. Her ogre of a boss being subservient?

Damned unsettling.

"What did you want to chat about?" Liberty said as soon as Jerome disappeared.

"Direct little thing, aren't you?"

Liberty tightened her lips and didn't respond.

"I just wanted to get to know you. After all, we're both—close—with Eli. I thought it would be good if we could be girlfriends."

"I'm not close with Eli, and I have enough girlfriends."

Grace tinkled a delighted laugh. "Oh, I'm not so sure about that. One of your 'friends' screwed your boyfriend."

Liberty widened her eyes. "How did you know that?" She hadn't told anyone on the island.

"Let's just say I do my homework when it comes to people Eli gets close to." She sipped her White Russian.

Jerome delivered Liberty's tea with a freakishly grateful smile.

"Thank you," she muttered.

"No, no. Thank you."

Liberty scowled at Grace. "Can you undo this please? He's giving me the willies. And I need to get back to work anyway."

"Not quite yet. Just a few more things. One, you don't have to look at me with such jealousy in those green eyes of yours. It's not like I'm the competition. Eli and I are just friends. Our—*intimate*—relationship ended years ago."

"What? I—I don't, *didn't* look at you like that. I could care less who Eli is intimate with."

She laughed again. "Come now, sweet cheeks. I wasn't born yesterday… wasn't turned yesterday either.

You have it bad for Eli." She leaned close and winked. "And I'll let you in on a little secret. Even if I were involved with Eli, you still wouldn't have to worry. Trust me, he's man enough for both of us."

Liberty's cheeks heated. She wanted to crawl under the table. "Uh, okay, thanks for the update." She stood. "But I really need to get back to work." She breathed a sigh of relief when the front door opened and Hannah and her grandparents came in. Not only was she glad to see them, they gave her a perfect excuse. "I have more customers."

Liberty started to walk away, but Grace gripped her wrist. Her fingers were strong, her skin soft… yet eerily cold.

"Last thing," Grace said in a low voice. "If you don't embrace your destiny. Truly embrace it, you'll never survive."

"I've embraced my—"

"No. No you haven't. You're still afraid. And your fear can get Eli killed. So, I want you to listen carefully. Whatever daddy issues you have are over. He's gone. He can't reject you again, so suck it up and stop being so afraid to fail, to disappoint him."

"That's ridiculous." Liberty had trouble speaking over the knot of anger in her throat. She didn't know how Grace knew so much, but she didn't know as much as she thought. "My dad didn't reject me. He sent me away because he loved me. He wanted to protect me."

The slow, feral smile appeared again. "Your head is telling you that, but what does your heart say about it?"

Liberty tugged on Grace's hold, and the she-vamp released her. Without replying, Liberty whirled and stalked over to Hannah's table. The young girl and her grandparents—Lester and Nelda Rankin—were from Oklahoma, and Liberty had grown attached to them in the few weeks she'd known them. It was comforting having a little piece of home in this new and sometimes frightening place.

"Hey guys." Liberty forced a smile. "How are things?"

"We're having a wonderful time," Hannah's grandmother said.

Hannah frowned. "It sucks, though, that summer's almost over, and we'll be leaving." She was thirteen, blonde, pretty. "I'll miss you, Liberty."

Affection squeezed Liberty's heart. "I'll miss you too. We'll Facebook and stay in touch. And when I go back home, I'll look you up."

Hannah's face lit with delight. "Promise?"

"Cross my heart." Liberty dragged her fingers in an X across her chest. "Now, what can I get for you?"

After they placed their order, Liberty was heading to the back when Hannah's voice spoke behind her. "Liberty, wait."

Liberty turned. She hadn't realized Hannah had followed her. "What's up?"

The girl's usually cheery features were drawn into a frown. "I was wondering... that cave of youth on the island?"

There was rumor that a cave on the island held water that promised eternal youth. It was a myth, but it kept tourists returning. In truth, the cave held holy water. "Yeah, what about it?"

Hannah glanced back at her grandparents. "Grandma and Grandpa are getting... old. Grandpa has heart problems. If anything happened to them, I don't know what I'd do. I might have to go live with my mom."

"Aw, honey. I'm sure they'll live a long time. But would living with your mom be all that bad?"

Hannah's eyes filled with tears, and she brushed them away. "You have no idea. I was wondering, will you help me find the cave of youth? If I could find it, my grandparents wouldn't have to die."

Liberty didn't know where the cave was located, but she knew it wouldn't help Hannah. "Oh, Hannah. You don't really believe in that nonsense do you?"

She shrugged. "I figure it's worth a try. So, will you help me?"

"I would love to, even though I don't believe in it, but things are kind of crazy for me right now, I really don't have time. Maybe later, in a week or two?"

Hannah's face crumpled in disappointment, but she nodded. "Sure, yeah. A week or two. Guess I'll let you get to work."

Guilt gnawed at Liberty, and she almost called Hannah back, told her she would help, but she had a vampire to hunt, and she didn't have time to waste on a child's ridiculous whims. She put it out of her mind and headed to the computer to place the Rankins' order.

****

Liberty hardly slept the night of Grace's visit to the tiki bar. She was sluggish the entire next day and couldn't wait to get home. As soon as she did, she lay down for a nap.

She'd just gotten into a deep sleep when she was awakened by Antoine. "You have company, Miss Van Helsing."

She blinked sleepily at the bedside clock. Eight p.m. She'd only been in bed for half an hour. She groaned and pushed the hair out of her face. "Who is it?"

"Eli."

She fell back onto the pillows. "You woke me for him?"

"It is my understanding that the two of you are to work together, is that not correct?"

"Yeah. It's correct."

"Shall I tell him to come back another time?" His mouth quirked. "Or shall I *try* to tell him? I am afraid Eli does not take orders very well."

"No, he definitely doesn't. Give me five minutes, and I'll be down."

"As you wish."

"And Antoine? Have a strong cup of coffee ready for me please."

"Of course."

In ten minutes instead of five, she'd brushed her teeth, washed her face, thrown on jeans and a Hard Rock Cafe t-shirt, but forced herself not to put on makeup. She wasn't out to impress Eli.

"What do you want?" she asked when she entered the kitchen. She turned her back to him and sipped the coffee Antoine had prepared.

"Uh, I think there's a matter of a little job we have to do. Finding the vampire and then you... I don't know, maybe slay him?"

Liberty took another gulp of the coffee. It burned her tongue but that was okay. It gave her something else to focus on besides the tension in every nerve of her body.

Feeling fortified by the strong coffee, she was ready to face Eli. "Any ideas on where to start?"

"I have a few places we can check out. Some vampire hangouts. We can ask questions. Ask if they

41

know of anyone acting 'off' lately."

"You mean more 'off' than your normal, average, demented vampire?"

He grinned. "Insults, Liberty? How are we ever going to make a team if you keep hurting my feelings?"

She barked a sarcastic laugh. "Show me some feeling before I'll believe I've hurt them."

He moved closer to her. So close she could see the black pupils in his shimmery silver eyes.

"What kind of feelings do you want me to show you?" He was doing that husky-voiced thing again that made shivers move over her flesh. "Kindness? Compassion?" He lifted his fingers and moved a strand of hair back from her face. "Desire?"

Something bloomed in her belly—something warm and pleasant and totally inappropriate. She growled and moved away from him. "You're going to have to knock that crap off if you expect me to work with you."

"What crap?" He lifted his eyebrows in mock innocence.

"That flirty, sensual, teasing, shallow crap."

He crossed his arms over his chest and cocked his head to the side. "Ah, so you find me sensual?"

She bit her lip and huffed out a breath. "Seriously, Eli. I need to know you'll behave. That you'll quit practicing your too obvious seduction routine on me. It comes off as cliché and insincere. The bimbos you pick up might fall for it, but it doesn't work on me." She slammed her coffee cup on the counter and turned to him, hands planted on her hips. "Now, are you going to cut the BS or do we call this whole thing off?"

The teasing light left his eyes. A muscle ticked in his jaw, and he gave a quick nod. "Sure. No problem. From now on, business only. I won't pull any more of that phony flirtation stuff with you. I'll save it for my bimbos."

She gave a curt nod back. "Thank you. Now, where to?"

"Bite Club. It's a vampire bar."

"*Bite* Club? Isn't that a little—obvious?"

"Maybe, but tourists don't seem to get it, so it doesn't really matter." He gestured with his head toward the door. "Come on. You can ride with me."

Chapter 5

The trip to the Bite Club was silent. Liberty bailed from Eli's Corvette and strode to the door, not waiting to see if Eli followed. When she went inside, she wished she *had* waited.

The bar was so dark, she could barely see in front of her, but splotches of red—splotches that looked like blood spatters on the walls—showed up in stark contrast.

Fear clutched her chest, and she tore her eyes away from all the red. She told herself it wasn't blood… it was only paint. She almost believed it.

Loud rock music by a band she didn't recognize blasted, and bodies were packed in tight. Dizziness assailed her, and nausea rose to her stomach. The only thing she could focus on was all the red…

"You okay?" Eli's low voice spoke into her ear.

She took a deep breath and nodded jerkily.

He slipped an arm around her waist. "This way. Don't worry. I've got you."

The tension inside her immediately eased. How could she find comfort with someone so dangerous, so untrustworthy? Maybe because he was the lesser of the current evils.

He led her to the bar and indicated the only available stool. She took it, and he stood next to her, his hip touching her knee. She moved away to break the contact. The knowing look he gave her told her it hadn't escaped his attention.

The bartender was a young, red-haired, pierced woman with a tattoo of a bat across her exposed stomach. Hmmm… vampire or human? It wasn't always easy to tell.

"What do you want to drink?" Eli shouted to Liberty above the noise.

"Whatever sweet white wine they have." She elevated her voice to respond.

He grinned, "You don't have to shout. Remember, I can hear you."

She flushed in embarrassment and nodded. Eli turned to the girl and gave their orders.

"So," Liberty pursed her lips. "Do you think the guy we're looking for is one of the Evil Ones?"

Eli shrugged. "Possibly, but could be from either side."

The drinks came and Liberty took a sip of the wine—sweet and delicious just the way she liked it. "Why would one of the vampires on our side do something so horrible? Aren't they the good guys?"

"Not necessarily. When a vampire turns a human, ninety-nine percent of the time, that human takes on that vampire's tendencies. For the most part, we have the same inclinations as our sire, but there are some anomalies. The vampire urges are pretty much the same—a hunger and desire to feed, but if a vampire is turned by one of the good guys, they don't inherit the desire to kill. If turned by an EO, however, they most definitely inherit that desire."

Liberty knew that, but hadn't really considered the big picture. She frowned. "And you were turned by an EO. So, you have those tendencies? Still?"

He grimaced. "I do. I have to fight the urges constantly. For all of us, it's in our nature to feed, but while your average vampire can control it most of the time, and only take enough to satisfy, an EO has the urge to kill, relishes in it. Desires it."

Chills raced over flesh. "The urge to… kill? You have that urge?"

"Yes, Liberty. The urge to feed and feed until I feel the life drain from my victim." He smiled with a hint of malice, as if he enjoyed shocking her. "I not only crave sustenance, but I crave the power that taking a life gives." He raised his glass to his lips and stared at her over the rim as he swallowed a drink of the scotch. "Does that make you fear me?"

Something in his expression told her the idea of her fear excited him. She cleared her throat and shook her head. "No, I don't fear you. I know you can control those urges." She gave him a saucy grin. "Besides, why would it scare me? You'd have to be completely insane to feed on me." She lifted her wine in a mock toast. "And you're only *partially* insane."

He chuckled. "Touché."

She considered what he'd told her for a moment. "So if vampires take on the traits of their sire, then we're dealing with an EO for sure, right?"

Eli shook his head. "When humans are turned—no matter which kind of vampire turns them—they retain many of their former traits. For example, if we turn a serial killer, then we have a serial killer vampire."

Icy fingers crawled up her spine. "You—you think we might be dealing with a serial killer turned vampire?" She shuddered.

"Not necessarily. I'm just making the point that we

don't know what kind of human this vampire was to begin with. So, he could be from either side."

Liberty took another sip of her wine. "Maybe we should investigate the new vamps that were turned."

"We could try, but there's not exactly a roster of recent recruits."

"Oh." Her cheeks warmed with embarrassment. Some investigator she was.

She was taking another sip of her wine, when someone on her left latched onto her arm. She whirled to find a hulking, tattooed vampire, fangs exposed, glaring down at her. His skin was a puckered gray, his eyes red and ferocious.

"Hey there, missy," he growled. "You are one fine ass, tasty-looking—"

Eli reached across her and latched onto the vampire's neck. "Back off, buddy."

Liberty scrunched against the bar to keep from being squashed by the pressure of Eli's body.

"Screw you," the vampire growled, his voice strangled from Eli's grip. "You bring a morsel like this in here, you gotta expect to share."

"Let her go, or I'll rip out your heart and feed it to you." Eli's voice was more deadly than the words he spoke. Liberty shivered.

The vampire's grip on her arm tightened. He lifted his free hand and latched onto Eli's wrist, but he couldn't budge his hold. His eyes went back to Liberty, then narrowed. "Wait," he croaked. "You're that Van Helsing chick."

Eli released him with a shove, and the vampire let go of Liberty simultaneously.

"That's right," Eli said. "Feast at your own risk."

The vampire retracted his fangs and chuckled, rubbing his neck. He looked down at Liberty. "You're not very smart. After what happened to your old man, I would think you'd wise up and get your ass as far from this island as possible. Are you that brave or just stupid?"

"What do you mean?" She turned to Eli. "What's he talking about? What happened to my father?"

Eli's jaw tightened. He took a drink of his scotch and glared at the vampire. "Get the hell out of here, before I make good on my promise."

The vampire drew back his shoulders, stared at Eli for a few moments, then backed away, disappearing into the crowd.

"Well?" Liberty demanded. "What happened to Victor?" When she'd arrived at the island her father was ill—near death. No one had explained exactly what was wrong with him. Dread pooled in her chest. Apparently, the reason was more sinister than she realized.

"Let's get out of here. I'll tell you all about it." Eli threw cash on the bar and took her elbow, guiding her through the crush of bodies.

Once outside, he shoved his hands in his pockets and leaned against the side of the building, looking down at his feet.

Liberty crossed her arms and waited.

After a while, he lifted his gaze to her. "There's something I didn't tell you."

"Ha, no kidding."

He didn't respond to her sarcasm. "If a Van Helsing is bitten by a vampire on a full moon, the bite is fatal. But they don't die right away. They suffer, sometimes for months, and die a slow, painful death."

Her first thought was abject fear. She'd hunted on a

full moon… that could have happened to her. And Eli just let her go out there, exposed to that kind of fate. As had Antoine and Ryan.

She shook her head. "You, Antoine, Ryan, knowing what could happen, you sent me out on a hunt without telling me about the risk?"

"First of all, Ryan didn't send you; he tried to keep you from going. Secondly, he didn't know what happened to Victor. Antoine and I did, but we discussed it and decided that if you knew the potential consequences, you'd likely go anyway. But with that on your mind, you might not be focused as you should. You might make a mistake that could get you killed."

She hated to admit it, but he had a point. She would have gone, even if she'd known the risk. As had her father. The thought made her heart clench with grief. "That's what happened to my father?"

Eli nodded. "Two full moons before you arrived, he was on a hunt. Victor was a phenomenal, highly skilled hunter. In his time on the island, the EO population had been cut by seventy-five percent. The residents and tourists were safer than they'd been in decades." He gave a wry chuckle. "Up until a year or so before his death, I was one of the EOs he was determined to annihilate." He shook his head. "But that's another story. On the night he was injured, Victor was tricked, ambushed by someone he thought he could trust. She trapped him in a cave, on the pretense of leading him to a group of EO's. Once inside, he was attacked, fatally bitten."

She pictured her father entering a dark, creepy cave where betrayal and death awaited. Sadness tightened her throat. "But why would a vampire bite him, knowing what would happen to them?"

"Apparently, this friend of your father's had charmed him, convinced him to sacrifice himself for the greater good. She was a beautiful woman; men would do anything to please her."

"Was my father in love with her? Is that why he trusted her?"

Eli smiled and shook his head. "Your father never loved a woman other than your mother."

The thought made her happy, and at the same time depressed. How awful it must have been for him to send his child and the love of his life away in order to protect them. She wished he hadn't. In spite of the danger, she believed they would have all been much happier if they'd remained a family, here on the island. But what was done was done.

Liberty lifted a hand and rubbed her forehead. "Then who was she, why did he trust her and care about her so much? And what happened to her? Where is she now?"

"She was a friend of your mother's. She'd been in love with Victor for years, and thought once your mother was gone, they'd hook up. It never happened. After so many years of rejection, she went a little nuts."

"Wow." Liberty took in a deep lungful of the ocean air. How much more was there to learn about this island and its inhabitants? About her family? "So where is she now? If she was in love with my father, surely she regretted what she did to him, especially when he died."

A cold smile touched his mouth. "She didn't have time for regrets. As soon as I learned what she'd done, I hunted her down and snapped her neck."

The words fell like a punch to her gut. "You killed her?"

He snapped his fingers. "Like that. But first, I fed on

her. No sense in letting a good meal go to waste."

Nausea rose to her throat. In spite of what the woman had done, Liberty couldn't imagine just snuffing out a life like that, with no regrets, no second thoughts. But then, Eli didn't exactly operate on the same code of morals as others. Even though he was avenging her father, the thought of his murdering a woman made her sick to her stomach.

"I think I'd like to go home now."

Eli pushed off the wall and shrugged. "No problem. It's not like we've accomplished anything tonight. I'm sure you're anxious to crawl into bed and brood about what a twisted son of a bitch I am."

"You must admit, you're not exactly… normal."

He stepped closer, captured her gaze with his. "No, I'm not. And I won't hesitate to do what needs to be done, in any situation. That's something you need to understand, Liberty. This island is not the place for squeamishness and delicate sensibilities. If you don't grow a pair and quit whining, you'll end up like your father, only a whole lot sooner."

Chapter 6

Liberty sighed as she took in the view. The descending sun glistened on the water, and an albatross flew low against the purplish sky. Evenings were gorgeous in Sang Croc, but they were also frightening. The vampires would be rousing from sleep. The tame ones and the wild ones. Maybe even the one she was hunting. Would he kill again tonight?

Guilt gnawed at her for taking an evening off. Eli hadn't been pleased when she told him she wouldn't be joining him on his investigation. He'd guessed she had plans with Ryan, which she had neither confirmed nor denied.

A native man wearing a headband made of leaves and bamboo shoots stood knee deep in the ocean and blew a conch shell.

"That's the 'party time' signal," Ryan told her. "Let's go, we wouldn't want to disappoint him."

He took her hand and tugged her along the sand. The beach was alight with colorful, glowing lanterns. Smoke curled from the ground where tables and chairs were grouped. She and Ryan stopped next to where Diego and Nadia sat.

"Have a chair," Diego said. "Hi Liberty." Diego was Ryan's roommate, a vampire who'd treated her with hostility when she first arrived. He'd since warmed up to her. His girlfriend, Nadia, not so much.

"You mind?" Ryan asked Liberty.

She did, but she refrained from admitting it. "Not at all. Thanks, Diego."

Nadia, a pretty Jamaican girl with gorgeous blue eyes and a bad attitude didn't acknowledge Liberty, but she smiled at Ryan. "Hello, Ryan. So happy you could make it."

Liberty and Ryan sat in the empty chairs. Liberty looked over to the source of the smoke and spotted what appeared to be a pit in the ground. "What's going on over there?"

"That's a ground oven," Diego said. "They lay fire wood inside with volcanic stones and cook meats, fruits, and vegetables wrapped in banana leaves, sometimes in baskets made from coconut leaves."

"Fascinating," Liberty said.

"And wicked yummo," Ryan added. "It's been cooking all day. Should be ready soon."

Liberty's stomach growled, even though she'd had a big lunch. The food sounded so enticing it made her hungry again.

"Let's go get the ladies a drink," Diego suggested.

Ryan stood. "We'll be right back."

She almost begged him not to go. Stuck here alone with Nadia sounded like pure torture. They worked together at the Getaway but managed to ignore one another most of the time. Now, that wasn't an option.

After several seconds of tense silence, Liberty summoned her courage and turned to Nadia. "Tell me something. Why don't you like me?"

Nadia's white teeth flashed in a derisive smile. "Everybody don' have to like everybody."

"No, they don't. But I would like to know how come

you don't like me."

Nadia lifted her brows. "Do you like me?"

The question took Liberty aback, and she didn't speak for a few moments. Finally, she said, "I really don't know you."

"Right. I don' know you eider. Less keep it dat way, cheerleader." She pronounced it *'chea-lea-dah.'*

Liberty chuckled. "Did you just call me cheerleader? If so, you've got it all wrong. I was never a cheerleader."

"No? Perhaps not. But I bet you date star football playah."

"Yes," Liberty admitted. "But he was a douche."

A slight smile touched Nadia's lips. Liberty counted that as a small step toward progress.

The guys returned with their drinks. Ryan handed Liberty a coconut shell with a straw sticking from it and pineapple and other fruits hanging on the side.

"What's this?" she asked.

"A Mahana. Try it."

She did, and almost moaned in ecstasy as the creamy pineapple-vanilla flavor filled her mouth. "Amazing." She took another long sip.

"Careful," Ryan said. "They don't taste that strong, but they'll knock you on your arse."

Everyone at the table laughed, including Nadia.

Liberty felt happy, light, carefree. She barely thought about the vampire she was hunting or about Eli. Fortunately, Eli was absent tonight, which definitely helped keep thoughts of him at bay.

Not long after they finished an amazing dinner, the show began. The first act was fire dancers—men twirling flaming torches. She'd seen the dance once before, but was as enthralled as she'd been then with the beauty and danger of the looping rings of fire.

Bianca and a guy Liberty had never seen before—a tall, dark-haired, guy with hazel eyes and the tanned body of a Greek god—stopped by the table.

"Hi guys, having fun?" Bianca asked.

"A blast." Liberty was on her third Mahana, and she noticed her words slurred a little. Maybe she'd better heed Ryan's advice.

Bianca introduced her date, Luciano Goode. "In a little while, the women will be dancing," Bianca said. "It's a free-for-all kind of thing where anyone can join." She looked at Nadia, then at Liberty. "You guys want to?"

"I have no idea how," Liberty said.

Bianca shrugged. "So you'll learn. I even have a costume for you."

"Uhm, I don't think—"

Nadia laughed. "The brave hunter afraid of a little dance?" There was challenge and a touch of hostility in her expression.

"I'm not afraid."

"Then what is stopping you?"

"Are you going to do it?" Liberty returned the challenge.

Nadia shook her head. "I know the dance. I have not'ing to prove."

Feeling trapped, Liberty nodded. "Sure, yeah. I'll give it a shot."

"Yes!" Bianca took Liberty's hand and pulled her to her feet. "You'll have so much fun." She turned to the 'too hot to be real' guy and said, "You sit with them. We'll be back after."

Liberty followed Bianca behind a curtain that had been constructed at the back of the stage.

Bianca dug around in her beach bag and pulled out a flowered bikini top and an emerald green rectangle of material. "Here's your top and a pareu, a wraparound skirt I have a shell necklace and a flower for your hair."

Liberty eyed the skimpy skirt with dismay. "You're kidding me, right?"

"No, it will be adorable on you. Trust me."

Liberty allowed Bianca to tie the skirt around her waist beneath her sun dress. Liberty turned her back and slipped the dress off, then put the bikini top on.

"Oh my God!" Bianca clapped her hands when Liberty turned to face her. "You look amazing."

The skirt brushed the tops of her thighs. She felt self-conscious, exposed. But Bianca, the tall, curvy brunette, looked like a model. Her pareu was a deep blue, and shorter than Liberty's, revealing a long expanse of tanned thigh. Liberty bit back a flash of envy and smiled. "I feel like an idiot, but you look amazing."

"Let's go knock their sandals off."

Liberty laughed and followed Bianca around the curtain and up onto the stage. She was relieved to find a group of twenty or so women in similar attire already on-stage. Maybe no one would notice her.

An island tune played and the women began to dance in sync. They shimmied their hips and gestured gracefully with their arms. Liberty had no idea how to emulate them.

"Here, I'll show you. Just watch me." Bianca stood by Liberty's side and made the same moves, only much slower than the other women. Liberty followed her lead and, in a few moments, the movement began to feel more comfortable.

"Now," Bianca said. "Widen your circle." Bianca placed her hands on Liberty's hips and moved them in wider arcs. "Close your eyes and feel the music. The rhythm tells you how to perform the dance."

Liberty obeyed, and in seconds, felt she had the dance down—at least somewhat. "Okay, I think I've got it." The booze had relaxed her enough that she was less self-conscious. She closed her eyes and swayed her hips to the music.

Once she felt more comfortable, she opened her eyes and looked out over the crowd—and locked eyes with Eli.

She caught her breath, missing a step and almost falling on her butt. He was staring straight at her, his eyes shimmering in the semi-darkness. The other dancers, the other people, the sounds, all faded from her consciousness. Her only awareness was of Eli… his captivating stare, his touch, the danger and excitement surrounding him that made her heart pump with excitement every time he was near…

She ceased that line of thinking. What was wrong with her? She had an amazing guy like Ryan and couldn't get over this unsettling pull toward Eli—a murderer, when it came right down to it.

The dance required a turn, and she executed it. When she faced back to the audience, Eli was gone. She tamped down her disappointment. His leaving was a good thing. Now she could enjoy the rest of her night without his disturbing presence. She sought out Ryan and found him still at the table, watching her with a rapt expression. Nadia and Diego had left.

The song ended, and Liberty started back stage.

"Where are you going?" Bianca asked.

"To change."

"Let's keep these on. Don't you love them?"

Liberty laughed. "They're fine for the stage, but I can't see myself running around the festival half—"

A growl ripped through the night, followed by a terrified female scream.

Liberty whirled to the source of the sound. Half a dozen men—vampires, Liberty guessed—were charging through the tables of party-goers, flipping tables on their end as they went. People screamed and many of them scattered.

"Where's Liberty Van Helsing?" one of the vampires shouted.

"Son of a bitch," Liberty muttered. She hadn't brought any weapons. Didn't think she'd need them on her night off from hunting, since Rupert called a truce.

She grabbed one of the posts buried in the ground at each corner of the stage. With bare feet, she kicked it in the same spot, over and over. Shards of pain shot through her foot, but in moments, the post cracked in two. One end was jagged, somewhat pointed. Not exactly a stake, but it would have to do.

She gripped it tightly in her hands, just as the group of vampires spotted her and headed her way.

"Oh, God, Liberty. Let's get out of here," Bianca's voice shook with terror.

"No, you go." Liberty kept her eyes on the vampires as she spoke to Bianca.

"I can't leave you."

"If you don't, you'll die. They can't kill me."

A vampire could only take the life of a Van Helsing on a full moon night. But they could damn sure cause her some pain. She didn't mention that to Bianca. "Get the hell out of here, now! I'll just have to worry about saving your ass while I fight them off."

Bianca let out a cry of frustration, but Liberty heard her footsteps as she fled.

The group of vamps stopped six feet in front of Liberty. The one in front, a stocky man with red hair and a goatee who seemed to be in charge, laughed. "Look here, boys. Little hunter girl thinks she's going to hurt us with that bit of kindling."

She wasn't sure how much she could hurt them, but maybe she could prevent them from harming anyone else. Worry for the others slithered through her. Where was Ryan? She didn't see him, but she couldn't take her eyes off the vampires to look for him.

"Just get the hell out of here and there won't be any trouble." She made her voice strong, even though she was trembling inside.

"Oh, but *trouble* is what we like. It's up to you how much. We're taking you back to Rupert, so you decide how painful the trip is going to be."

She forced a cocky smile. "That depends on how much pain you can take."

The amusement left his face. He opened his mouth, but before he could speak, she said, "Why do you *think* you're taking me back to Rupert? He called a truce."

"Yeah, but we still know he'd like to get his hands on you. This way, it's on us, not him, truce intact."

While he'd been speaking, a tall, lanky vampire with a bar piercing in his ear had circled around and was trying to get in position behind Liberty.

Without stopping to think, she lunged and drove the makeshift stake into his chest, through his heart. With a grunted *oomph*, he dropped to the ground. He bubbled into a pile of smoldering ash at her feet.

She whipped back toward the remaining four vampires. The red-haired one looked even paler than vampires normally did.

"Unless you want the same—" She halted. Ryan was approaching the vampires from the rear. Panic for him paralyzed her for a moment. He wielded a flaming torch over his head and brought it down on one of the vampire's back. The vampire let out an agonized scream and crumpled to the ground. He wouldn't be down long. Ryan hadn't killed him—he'd only incapacitated him momentarily.

One of the other vampires reached out for Ryan, grabbing him by the front of his shirt and lifting him off his feet.

Liberty's paralysis broke. "No," she shouted. "Let him go."

"What is the meaning of this?" A man's voice cut through the melee.

Liberty looked over her shoulder to find Rupert and Blake standing among the debris that had once been tables and chairs. Rupert's handsome face was dark with anger.

The vampires halted as if of one mind. The oaf holding Ryan flung him to the ground.

Liberty cried out and ran to Ryan's side and dropped to her knees beside him. "Are you okay?"

He blinked, then grimaced, but nodded. "Knocked the wind out of me, but I'm fine." He looked up at her and flashed a smile. "How about you?"

"Peachy. Come on, let's get you up."

The vampires were all looking uncertainly at

Rupert.

"Just what do you imbeciles think you're doing?" Rupert's voice held barely suppressed rage.

The red-haired vampire stepped forward. "We were capturing her." He gestured toward Liberty. "For you. What's the problem?"

"The *problem* is, for one, you are to follow my orders, and I did not order you to capture Miss Van Helsing."

"We didn't want anyone to get hurt. We were just going to bring the girl back to you."

Rupert glanced down at the still smoldering vampire. "Guess your little plan didn't work out like you intended." He turned a look on the vampire that made him visibly shrivel. "Secondly, we have called a truce. I do not want this girl harmed in any way. Nor do I want her taken hostage. Until this rogue is caught, we are at peace with the humans." Rupert moved closer to the red-haired vampire. "I want each of you to know now, that I will stand for no insubordination. Until I declare differently, all humans—other than those that already belong to us—are off limits. After all, how will we be able to tell you apart from the murdering animal out there if you behave just like him?"

The vampire dropped his head. "I guess we wouldn't."

"Correct."

He walked over to Liberty. His eyes raked her body, and she resisted the urge to cover herself with her hands.

"Perhaps you should put something on, my dear. I can quell their desire for blood, but I am not certain if I can prevent them from giving in to—other desires."

Her skin heated. She sensed movement behind her

and looked over her shoulder. Ryan approached with a table cloth and draped it over her shoulders, pulled it together in front of her. She gave him a look of gratitude.

"I'll handle that," Ryan said through gritted teeth.

"See that you do, my boy. We wouldn't want our little hunter to be defiled."

"No, we definitely wouldn't want that," Liberty muttered. She wrapped the tablecloth around her more tightly and looked up at Rupert. "What did you mean earlier, humans that already belong to you?"

"There are some humans who have joined us on our side of the island. We take good care of them, and they take good care of us, if you get my meaning."

"I do. I assume they are not there willingly?"

He shrugged. "Some are. Not all. Why? Are you formulating a plan to rescue them? If so, I would get that out of your mind, little hunter. You have no idea of the type of fortress I have built. You would deeply regret trying anything foolish, as would those you care about. I have very—painful, yet effective ways of exacting justice on those who try to thwart me."

She lifted her chin as if his threat didn't make her knees weak. "If you have them to feed on, why bother with tourists and other humans?"

His smile didn't reach his eyes. "You have heard variety is the spice of life, have you not? Besides, we cannot feed to our fill on the limited supply we now have. We must give them time to recover between feedings."

Nausea knotted her chest. He spoke of those poor people like they were sub human—*things* to satisfy his disgusting whims.

He looked at Ryan over Liberty's shoulder. "See that she gets home okay." He turned his gaze to Liberty.

"I apologize for the behavior of my vampires. It won't happen again."

"You might be sure you see to that." Her words were braver than she felt. "I have some special ways of exacting justice myself."

Liberty and Ryan turned away, but Rupert's voice stopped them. "The truce is only until after we catch this rogue vampire. Then, all bets are off."

Chapter 7

Liberty changed from her dance costume back into her dress, then she and Ryan helped the workers clean up the beach.

"Where did Diego and Nadia go?" Liberty asked.

Ryan shrugged. "They got into this huge fight and took off."

"I imagine it's not easy to get along with Nadia."

"She's not a bad sort, just takes some getting used to."

"Right." Liberty laughed. "Sort of like trying to get used to a Tarantula."

Ryan chuckled. "Not quite that bad."

After they were finished, Ryan insisted she come home with him. He wanted to make sure she was safe. She was more pissed than frightened, but she wouldn't say no to hanging with Ryan for a while instead of going to that huge house where she and Antoine were the only occupants.

Diego was at Ryan's bungalow when they arrived, but Nadia wasn't with him.

She and Ryan settled on the sofa, each with a beer. Diego drank whisky straight from a bottle.

"Rough time lately, mate?" Ryan asked.

"Just family stuff. And Nadia."

"What happened between you two?"

Diego grunted and took another swig of the whisky.

"She thought I was looking at Bianca when she was dancing."

"Were you?"

Diego grinned. "Sorry, bro. I know she's your sis, but she's a babe."

Ryan frowned. "Yeah, bucko. She *is* my sister."

"No offense. I really do love Nadia, but the chick's got a chip on her shoulder. You never know what's going to set her off. It's like being in a relationship with a viper."

Liberty smiled. "I was thinking Tarantula, but I'm sure viper works."

Diego scowled at her, then laughed. "You're not wrong." He chugged from the bottle again. "They say there aren't any poisonous spiders or snakes in French Polynesia, but they've never met Nadia."

Ryan chuckled. "Sorry about all that, mate."

"Oh well, it's my problem." Diego put down his whisky and walked toward the door.

"Going out?" Ryan asked. "You're not driving, are you?"

"Yes to going out, no to driving. I need to grab some fresh air." He grinned. "Don't act like you'll miss me. It will give you two some alone time."

"Thanks. And don't worry, I won't act like I'll miss you."

Diego winked and headed out the door.

After he left, Ryan tugged Liberty to his side and whispered, "I almost went crazy when I thought they were going to hurt you."

She laughed softly. "Me too."

His hands cupped her face, his eyes gleaming like black onyx. "You're beautiful in the candlelight."

Her heartbeat accelerated, cutting off her breath. She forced a chuckle. "Not so much in the bright lights, huh?"

He didn't smile. Electricity zipped through the air. He bent his head and touched his lips to hers.

She melted into him with a sigh, returning the kiss. Although it seemed cliché, her blood literally sang through her veins. Was this it? Was this what love felt like? She didn't know, but she knew she wanted to be closer to Ryan. As close as a man and woman could get.

He rested into the corner of the sofa and pulled her on top of him, then slid his hands down to her hips, pressing her more tightly to him.

Excitement sang through her blood as hot desire pulsed over her skin. *It's time. This is it.*

She slipped her tongue inside his mouth and tangled her fingers in his hair. He tasted of beer and toothpaste, a pleasant, heady mixture.

He groaned deep in his throat and pulled her shirt loose from her jeans. Then his warm, strong hands were on her flesh, sliding along her ribs, to the undersides of her breasts. His fingers slipped beneath the straps and stroked her… right there…

"Ryan," she breathed against his mouth.

"Hmmm?" His fingers slowed but didn't still. They made lazy circles along her breasts, causing an ache deep within her. An ache she was ready to have assuaged.

"Let's go to the bedroom."

He stilled and gently pushed her away from him. Heaving a deep sigh, he rose and scooted the edge of the sofa. He rubbed his hands vigorously over his face.

"What's wrong?" Her voice came out shakily.

"I—I can't."

"What?" He was rejecting her? "You don't want to…" In spite of her brazen actions, she couldn't make herself say the words.

He gave a lopsided grin. "Oh, sweetheart, you have no idea how much I want to."

"Then what?"

"You. You're not ready."

"Yes, yes I am. I'm so ready." The tingle of desire had waned, but not completely disappeared. With another touch, she'd be a raging inferno of yearning. "Come on. Please." She summoned her courage. "Make love to me."

He looked at her. "You're a virgin, am I right?"

She pursed her lips in irritation. "What's that got to do with it?"

"Your first time should be special, magical." He searched her eyes as if in question. "With someone you love."

"But I—" She'd been about to say she loved him. But did she really? She wasn't sure enough to say the words.

"See. You can't say it, can you?"

"I care about you. A lot. I've never felt this way about anyone."

"That's nice, Liberty. But I *love* you."

She froze, not sure how she felt about his declaration. He'd told her before that he thought he was falling in love with her, but this was the first time he'd actually said the words.

A part of her was thrilled. The other part—terrified. She strengthened her resolve. The terrified part would have to take a hike, her girl parts had priority.

"You love me? Then that's all that matters. It's right,

Ryan. I know it is."

He leaned forward and placed a gentle, almost brotherly, kiss on her lips. "When you can say the words. When you can tell me you love me and really mean it. Then you'll be ready."

She bit back tears. *Damn, damn, damn.* Couldn't a girl just get laid? She jumped to her feet and snatched her purse from the couch. "Take me home please."

"Liberty, don't be angry, love. Doesn't it count for something that, as much as I want you right now, I'm considering your feelings? That I respect you enough to wait?"

She was aware she was being childish, but at that moment she didn't care. "Later it might count for something. But right now, it just feels like a slap in the face."

He winced. "I'm sorry. Truly. But you'll be ready one day. You'll be madly in love with no hesitation. Then it will be the right thing. When that time comes, I hope I'm the lucky guy."

An unwanted image of Eli flashed in her mind. She pushed it away as quickly as it came. "I hope you are too," she whispered.

Chapter 8

The next night, Liberty met Eli at the beach.

"Ready?" he asked, a smile hovering on his mouth.

"You act as if we're out for a night of fun. We're hunting a killer, you know."

"Sure, I know. But don't you think that's loads of fun?"

"You're twisted."

"Thank you."

She clenched her lips and stomped up the beach. "Where to?"

"I say we just hang out in town, keep our eyes open. You know, pretend we're out for a good time. If we see anything out of place, suspicious, we'll check it out."

"So we just sit around and wait for this maniac to target another girl?"

"If you have a better idea, I'm all ears."

She didn't, so she let Eli guide her to a club a few doors down from Perfect Getaway. This one catered to tourists rather than vampires. Good choice. It was unlikely their guy would be cruising vampire bars to find his human victims. Both the dead girls had been drinking the night they died. The latest one was killed on the beach, but the first victim had been picked up in a bar.

Inside, loud music played and even louder voices nearly drowned it out. She followed Eli to the bar. There were no seats, so they were forced to stand between people, too damn close together.

"The lady will have a white wine, and I'll have a scotch on the rocks," he told the bartender.

"You didn't bother to ask me what I wanted?" Liberty snapped.

His brows lifted. "If I had, what would you have ordered?"

She hesitated for a few seconds, then muttered, "White wine." Before coming to the island, she hadn't been much of a drinker. Her boyfriend—ex-boyfriend, Cam—and her other friends drank a lot, but it never appealed to her. Partly because she was underage—she'd never been much of a rebel. But since coming to the island where the drinking age was eighteen, she'd discovered a fondness for alcohol. Especially wine.

Eli handed her the drink, then leaned his back against the bar.

"Crowded." He took a sip of his scotch.

"Observant," she replied churlishly.

He chuckled. "Seriously? Can you really not spend five minutes in my presence without your claws coming out?"

He had a point. If they had to work together, she could at least be mature—civil. "Sorry," she mumbled.

He cupped a hand to his ear. "What was that? I didn't quite catch it."

"Liar. I know about your super vampire hearing. You just want me to say it again." She sipped her wine. "Not going to happen. I almost choked on it the first time."

He inclined his head. "I'll accept the first apology then."

They fell silent, their gazes going around the room.

The place was probably too crowded. Doubtful the vampire would snatch someone from a busy nightclub. But then, if he'd picked his first victim up, and she'd gone willingly, he could discreetly take her from right under their noses. And then attack her…

A shudder ran through Liberty.

"You okay?" Eli turned those brilliant, devastating icicle eyes on her.

"I'm fine. Just a little freaked out that this guy could be here this very second. Could be taking a girl out to slaughter as we stand here enjoying our drinks."

He quirked a smile. "So you're enjoying yourself, are you?"

"The *drink*. I said I was enjoying the drink."

The smile remained. He lifted his glass in a toast and downed the liquor. "To good drinks, then. And a good team who will, from this point forward, refrain from bitchy comments."

"By bitchy comments, I assume you're referring to me. What's your end of the bargain?"

"No more flirting, remember? Hadn't you even noticed? I've barely looked your way all evening. I haven't ogled your breasts, or touched your hair." His voice lowered. "Or moved so close to you I could smell your blood, feel your heartbeat."

In spite of her attempts at indifference, his words sent a shiver over her skin. "Yes, I noticed," she croaked. She took another sip of wine and cleared her throat. "Thank you."

"No problem. I know how much you despise insincere flirting."

She nodded and downed her wine. She was glad he'd knocked the seduction act off, wasn't she? Then why did she feel just a slight tremor of disappointment?

Uhm, maybe because she was slutty? Last night, she'd practically begged Ryan to have sex with her, and this evening, she was halfway wishing Eli *would* flirt, maybe a little more than halfway, like at least three quarters.

She tried to put it out of her mind the rest of the evening and focus on the task at hand—catching a murderer.

They hit two more bars, drank a few more drinks, hung out for a few more hours, and not one sign of the vampire.

She was definitely feeling the effects of the wine. For a person new to the drinking scene, she'd certainly put several away.

After the bars closed and the streets emptied of people, Liberty and Eli walked back down the beach to the lot where their cars were parked.

She stumbled and Eli took her elbow, helping her stay upright. "Watch it now. I think you're toasted."

She rubbed her cheek and shook her head. "No, just tired."

"You're bombed out of your mind. In our future outings, we should leave alcohol alone. If you did run into our mystery maniac, he'd have you shredded to ribbons in no time."

For some reason, that struck her as hilarious. She stopped walking and doubled over with giggles.

Eli took her shoulders and lifted her to face him. "What's so damned funny? I'm serious."

That made her laugh even harder. "You—you're the one—" She gasped between bursts of laughter, trying to catch her breath. "You're the one who's—" She laughed some more. "Trying to be serious? That's a switch, am I right or am I right?"

He snorted in irritation. "Wasted is what you are. For God's sake, a newbie drunken hunter. Exactly what we need to take down this asshole."

"Sorry," she slurred, trying to focus, to sober up. "You're right. No way would I be any goodn' this con-con-dishen."

He scowled. "Apology accepted. Second apology, I might add."

She smiled. For some reason his reminder didn't bother her. She poked a finger against his chest. "Don't get used to it, bucko."

He wrapped his fingers around hers, held on for a split second, then released her. "Come on, I'll drive you home."

"I took—I mean brought—my car. I can drive."

"No way in hell am I letting you get behind the wheel. Lover boy can bring you to get your car tomorrow."

She scowled, but Eli was right. She didn't want to kill someone—or herself.

Just before they reached the parking lot, they passed a tiare shrub blooming with white flowers. "These are gorgeous." She inhaled the fragrant scent. "And they smell amazing." She turned a delighted smile on him. "Can I pick one?"

"Of course. The natives of Sang Croc want people to enjoy the beauty of their flora. The motto is, there are always more to grow." He stopped and gripped a flower by its stem, pulling it from the bush. "Here you go."

She hadn't realized he'd moved, but suddenly he was close. Their bodies almost brushed. She didn't remind him of the rules about no flirting. If she did, she was afraid he'd step away. He locked his eyes on hers and lifted the flower, gently tucking it behind her ear.

She swallowed hard and took a shallow breath. His eyes dropped to her mouth. Involuntarily, her lips parted.

He was going to kiss her… and she was pretty certain she going to let him. Even in her drunken state, she vowed she wouldn't go as far as she'd wanted to go with Ryan. But she wanted to kiss Eli—had wanted to since she'd first seen him.

They'd come close a few times, but something had always interrupted them. Tonight, there were no distractions. She'd had enough to drink that she didn't feel her normal inhibitions. But she couldn't use the booze as an excuse. Her adrenaline was pumping, and she'd sobered considerably. Would she or wouldn't she? Would it be disloyal to Ryan? They hadn't exactly made a commitment, she hadn't told him she—

"Are you and Ryan a couple?" Eli asked.

She blinked, not sure she'd heard correctly. "Do what?"

"Are you and Ryan a couple?"

"That's not—not really your business."

"I need you to tell me that you are."

She frowned and put a hand to her forehead. "What?" He wasn't making any sense, and her head was fuzzy.

He stared down intently at her, his gaze roaming over her features. His voice was low in the hushed night. "If you say you're not, I'll do something stupid. If you belong to Ryan, tell me you do, and hands off."

She didn't answer. For several seconds.

His lips tightened. The two of them remained

sheltered in silence in the darkness. It was so quiet, she could hear the ocean waves lapping the sand.

He took the flower from her right ear and moved it to her left. He trailed his fingers along her cheek, making goose bumps break out over her flesh. "There you are. Left side."

"Left side?" Her throat was so dry, she could barely speak.

He nodded. "It means you're taken. Now all the guys will know you belong to Ryan, and they'll stay away."

She clenched her teeth, angry at herself for feeling disappointed, angry at him for not giving her what she wanted. Rejected by two guys in two nights.

Screw this romance crap.

****

Liberty was in a pissy mood the next night at work. It didn't improve when, just before closing time, the door opened and Rupert walked in.

"May I have Liberty's section?" he asked the hostess, keeping his gaze on Liberty.

"Certainly, right this way." The traitor picked up a menu and led him to one of Liberty's tables.

"Will this be okay, sir?" she asked.

"This will be delightful."

The hostess walked away, and Liberty reluctantly approached his table.

Rupert smiled up at her. "How are you this evening, my dear?"

"Why did you ask for my section?"

He gave her a wounded look. "I enjoy your company. I feel a certain… closeness to you."

"Really?" She shook her head. "Even though you

sent vampires to kidnap me not long after I arrived? Twice."

"Ah yes, that business before the truce." He shook a napkin out on his lap. "I will admit, I want to own you. But I admire you a great deal, if that takes the sting out of it."

"*Own* me? You're kidding, right?"

"Not at all. Rest assured, though, I meant what I said about calling a truce. Just until we resolve the pesky matter of the rogue vampire determined to ruin things for all concerned. But yes, I do want to own you. You could be of great value to me."

In spite of the absurdness of the conversation, she was curious. "How is that?"

"Your blood is quite… special."

"You mean deadly?" She tried to put a threatening note in her voice.

"Deadly, yes. Although not to everyone. And not with an antidote."

She frowned. "What are you talking about?"

"How much do you know about the Van Helsing lineage?"

Sadness weighted her heart. She'd planned on long talks with her father about that very thing. But he died shortly after she arrived on the island. She'd learned nothing.

She shrugged. "I know that Van Helsing was a hunter—a fictitious hunter I'd believed until I came here and found out the truth—that not only was he real, but I'm one of his descendants. Other than that, I know nothing."

"Then allow me to enlighten you. Sit, please."

She rolled her eyes. "What is it with vampires and

their oblivion to the fact that I have a *job* here? I can't just sit down any time. Besides, I wouldn't want to sit with you anyway."

"Don't you want to know more about your past? Your heritage?"

She did. Desperately. But surely she could learn it elsewhere. She didn't want to spend any more time than necessary in this monster's presence. On the other hand... he was here, he was offering...

"Bianca?" Liberty looked over her shoulder to where Bianca was wiping down one of her tables. "Can you cover my tables for a few minutes?"

Bianca waved her hand. "No problem."

Jerome wasn't in, so she wouldn't get her butt reamed for taking a break. She sat in a chair across from Rupert. "So, tell me."

"May I have a drink first? A martini, dry."

She sighed and went to the bar to get his drink. Diego was bartending. Ryan was off tonight, and she found herself missing him. Odd. She'd never been *that* girl. The clingy type who needed to be around her guy all the time. But Ryan made her feel... happy... cherished. She was lonely here without her family— maybe she was just craving some kind of connection.

She brought back the martini and placed it in front of Rupert, then took her chair once more. He sipped from the glass and sat it down, raising his gaze to her.

"Delicious. Thank you."

She didn't respond. She waited.

After a few moments, he said, "Abraham Van Helsing was born in the early 1800's. Up until that time, vampires roamed free and unchallenged, other than from the occasional stake to the heart. Van Helsing was born with a rare blood type—so rare, he was the first—and only person—documented to have it. Although his parents didn't share his blood type, he and his descendants did."

One day when Abraham was a boy, ten years old or so, he was out gathering fire wood when he was attacked by a vampire. The vampire drank from him, but didn't drain him. Something odd began to happen. The vampire released Abraham and stalked toward a jagged tree stump where he purposely impaled himself. Abraham was frightened, of course, but also felt a sense of power. Word spread, and vampires began to fear him, yet at the same time wanted him dead. Abraham's dad was a soldier—a strong, skilled, fierce soldier. He trained Abraham to be a vampire hunter."

As it turned out, Abraham's blood gave him special gifts that other humans didn't have. Over the years, they learned more about those gifts—one is a super human strength that you probably haven't even tapped into yet, the natural skill with weapons, and quickness—not unlike vampires. Also, they learned that the same blood that was fatal to vampires was healing to humans, and that Van Helsing blood had special properties that could actually benefit vampires."

Abraham married and had children, those children married and reproduced, so on and so forth. However, the Van Helsings of the past few decades have run into some unfortunate luck. Your father was the only surviving Van Helsing. He moved to this island when he was a teen. The island was inhabited by vampires, thanks to yours truly. I came here in the early 1900's and established my society. When your father arrived on Sang Croc, we were a powerful force. We ruled the island. Your father changed that. He was skilled, clever, courageous. He whittled the vampire population down to a fraction of its former numbers. So we had to begin exercising caution. Then we realized that if we would resist our urges to a degree, we could enjoy the bounty of new blood. Tourists would flock to the island, and we could selectively feast without killing off the entire human species and discouraging new humans from visiting."

She shook her head. She'd learned more in five minutes from her arch enemy than she had from her father, Antoine, Ryan, and Eli combined. "So what about the antidote, the potential benefits of my blood to vampires. I've never heard anything about that."

"A vampire who was also a scientist created an antidote to the lethal properties in your blood. If you take the antidote, your blood is not only safe to vampires for a period of time—it also allows us to see our reflection. The antidote in your blood and the ability to see our reflection wears off after a period of time—how long we haven't been able to pinpoint thus far—but the promise of having that ability makes it worth the risk."

"You—vampires—can't see your reflection?" The concept was hard to absorb. "How do you shave?" she blurted.

He threw his head back and roared with laughter. When he sobered, he said, "That is actually a logical question. It takes a lot of practice and some painful nicks, but we all learn."

"Why is seeing your reflection such a big deal? Why is it so desirable?" She couldn't believe she was actually having a conversation with this man. But she was fascinated by the details he was sharing and thirsty for more. Especially since this antidote directly affected her.

His expression softened, became almost wistful. "You wouldn't understand unless you were afflicted with this curse. Being unable to see your reflection—ever—gives one a sense of non-existence. That probably doesn't make sense to you, but to never have that confirmation of yourself looking back at you. That assurance that you are real—that you have sustenance—can be debilitating. We try not to focus on it, but the promise of that gift—to see oneself, to see what others see when they look at us, is priceless."

"So if you can't see your reflection, why is Eli so convinced he's a stud?"

Rupert chuckled. "The way women react to him gives him a pretty good indication."

Liberty rolled her eyes. "Where and what is this antidote? And how does a Van Helsing take it? How does it affect us when we do?"

He smiled a genuine smile, making his handsome features even more attractive. "My, you are a curious little cat, aren't you?" He took another sip of his martini. "The antidote is difficult to find. Only a few people are in possession of it. The scientist who created it sealed his formula and locked it away. No one knows exactly where. But a few vials were discovered in the late 1800's. As far as how you ingest it, you simply drink the potion. I do not know the precise effects it has on a Van Helsing. Various accounts have circulated over the years ranging from a state of pure nirvana to a brief bout with insanity. Perhaps different Van Helsings experience different results."

She sat back in her chair and shook her head. "Wow."

"Yes, it is a great deal to take in. But I thought you should have the whole story."

She harrumphed. "Apparently you're the only one who thinks that. My father, Antoine, Eli, Ryan, none of them bothered to enlighten me."

"They are trying to protect you."

"Right. Eli protecting me."

He smiled a knowing smile. "You really have no concept of who Eli is, how he feels, do you?"

She shifted in her chair and purposely avoided answering. "So you said there are only a few antidotes in existence. Do you know where they are right now?"

"Unfortunately, I do not. I have been searching for centuries."

"You never explained why you wanted to 'own' me. What good would my blood do you without the antidote?"

"If I do not find the antidote, your blood would still be useful to me. I would use it to punish those who defy me."

Horror and revulsion washed over her. "You would feed your own people my blood to punish them?"

"Absolutely. There is no better way than by example to ensure complete obedience. But do not fear, you would be treated well while in captivity. I am not a complete monster."

I beg to differ. She didn't say the words aloud. She wouldn't rock the boat while he was in a jovial non-violent frame of mind. "Would it really be worth it to capture me, risk your life and other lives attempting to do so, just to have a way to punish your followers? I'm sure a vampire with your capacity for evil has all sorts of cruel, effective ways to make them suffer."

"Thank you, my dear." His face lit up like she'd just crowned him King.

"That wasn't a compliment."

He chuckled. "Not to you, perhaps." He leaned forward and crossed his hands atop the table. "To answer your question, while I feel having you for my own would be worthwhile even if I never found the antidote, I fully intend to obtain the potion. Something you might not know about me is that I am an optimist. Not only that, when I want something, I get it. I want you, and I want the antidote. I shall have both."

"Is that a threat?"

"Not to be cliché, my dear, but you can consider it a promise."

Chapter 9

The next day was Liberty's day off. After much soul searching and internal arguing, she logged onto the computer in Victor's office. She hadn't been on Facebook since she'd come to the island. Other than the twice a week phone calls with her mother, she had no connection to her old life.

When her Facebook page came up, her heart squeezed. She had a message from Alyssa. They'd been best friends since third grade, until graduation night when Liberty had found her in bed with Cam. Liberty had lost a best friend and a boyfriend that night. Shortly after, she'd come to the island.

Funny how things had changed since then. Her heartbreak seemed so insignificant now, although she did miss Alyssa. They were like sisters. Liberty would never find another friendship like she had with Alyssa. She liked Bianca, and she'd made a few acquaintances since coming here that might lead to a close bond, but there was nothing like a lifelong best friend.

Liberty took a deep breath and began to read.

Liberty, I don't know what to say. I can't believe I'm even messaging you. I know you probably won't respond, but I had to reach out. I am so, so sorry for what I did. It was horrible and wrong, and I don't blame you for hating me. But I still love you. I miss you and I can't imagine never speaking to you again. Remember when we used to hang out at the arcade? I went there the other day and just sat and cried. Nothing is the same here without you. It sucks big time. I haven't even spoken to Cam since you left. We threw away something precious for one foolish mistake. You're the best friend a girl could have and I destroyed that. I hope your new life in paradise is as perfect as you deserve. One of these days, if you can find it in your heart to forgive me, I would love to speak to you… I would love to see you. Find out what you've been up to. Have you met a guy? Someone who treats you better than the a-hole Cameron? Haha, listen to me. I have a lot of room to talk. I hope you've found a better friend than I was to you.

Always your BFF,

Alyssa.

PS. I never take off my half of the friendship necklace. I would imagine you threw yours away. I don't blame you.

Tears were rolling down Liberty's cheeks by the time she finished the message. She wiped them away, but more took their place. In all the homesickness she'd suffered, none had been as severe as what she felt now. She wanted to see Alyssa, to share everything that had happened since she'd come to the island.

Alyssa was mistaken about the friendship necklace. Liberty had kept it, and in spite of what Alyssa had done, she cherished the keepsake—cherished their friendship. Her hurt and anger seemed foolish now. Yes, Alyssa had betrayed her, but everyone deserved a second chance. No one was perfect, and Liberty had learned that in a big way since coming to the island, especially about herself. And God, she missed Alyssa. Missed talking to her.

After a brief hesitation, she began to type. There was

no way she could tell Alyssa about the vampires, or about learning she was a Van Helsing, but she could fill her in on the surface details.

She wrote in the note that she forgave her, that she missed her. She wrote about her job, about Ryan and the other people she'd met—although she didn't mention Eli. She wasn't even sure how to put that into words. Not without mentioning the vampire thing.

Liberty told her about the beauty of the island and how she would love for Alyssa to visit. She hit reply, then immediately regretted it. Although she would like nothing more than to see Alyssa, did she really want her to come here? To try to keep the secrets of the island hidden? Or worse, get her best friend hurt—maybe killed? Alyssa wouldn't come, though. That was crazy. It was so expensive, so far away… There was nothing to worry about.

She hoped.

****

That night, Liberty met Bianca for drinks at Steamy Nights. Ryan had to work, and Bianca insisted on a girls' night out.

Liberty had fun, and even danced with a couple of guys, but none of them piqued her interest. Maybe she wasn't such a slut after all.

"You've got it bad, don't you?" Bianca said above the noise of the crowd.

"I've got what bad?"

Bianca grinned and took a sip of her drink. "The love bug, silly. You've barely given any of these blokes a second look. Even the head-turners."

Liberty's face heated, and she tried to hide it by taking a drink of wine. "I'm just not a big flirt."

"No, you're smitten, no doubt. The question is, who's the lucky guy? My brother… or Eli?"

"Ha," Liberty barked a laugh, but it sounded forced. "I can't *stand* Eli."

"Right. Sure. That's why you look at him like he's a chocolate truffle wrapped in fourteen-karat gold. I can't blame you. He is a tasty morsel. But so dangerous." She shuddered. "I wonder if having a go at that would be worth the risk."

Liberty's face warmed further. "Can we please not talk about this?"

Bianca's beautiful features lit up, and she laughed with glee. "Getting hot and bothered are we?"

Liberty downed the remainder of her wine. "I'm actually getting kind of tired. Can we go?"

"The night's still young. I didn't mean to spoil it. I was teasing."

"No, it's not that. I have to open in the morning. I'd really just like to go. If you want to stay, I'll go on without you." They'd driven separately for just that reason.

"I'll come along. It wouldn't be any fun by myself. Then I'll just look desperate and pathetic. Not to mention easy." Bianca winked. "And truth is, out of all of those, I'm only easy."

Liberty smiled. She wished she could be as relaxed, as nonchalant about sex as Bianca. But then, she didn't have the experience Bianca had.

They walked out into the balmy night. A half-moon hung low in the sky. Only a few weeks until the next hunt. She'd thought she would get a break between full moons, but that hadn't quite worked out. Rupert's words about her supposed strength, quickness, and natural skill came to mind. Maybe the gene had skipped her, because she certainly hadn't seen it. Although, she had broken the post at the festival. Not all girls could do that. Maybe she was developing those traits after all.

Liberty said goodnight to Bianca, then climbed into her Corolla and drove from the parking lot.

The road was shadowed in darkness, the overhang of trees blocking out the moon's glow.

As she was taking a curve in the road, a flash of something pale off to the side caught her attention.

She peered into the trees in time to see a young blonde girl disappearing into the shrubs. Hannah?

Liberty whipped the car to the side of the road and bailed out, hurrying to where she'd seen the girl.

"Hannah?" Liberty called. "Is that you?"

No answer for several seconds. Liberty shouted once more.

"Liberty?" the small voice came from ahead and to her left.

Liberty headed that direction, relief flooding her when she spotted Hannah. She wore jeans, a pink baby doll shirt, and tennis shoes. Her hair was pulled back in a ponytail. She looked closer to eight than fourteen.

Liberty rushed over and took Hannah's upper arms in her hands.

"Hannah, you can't be out like this. It's not safe." A few weeks ago, Hannah had snuck out of her hotel room and gone partying. She'd shown up at Liberty's door and been attacked by a vampire. Eli had mesmerized her into forgetting. Maybe that was a bad idea. A healthy dose of fear might do the impetuous girl some good.

Hannah sniffed. "My grandpa is getting sicker. I have to find the cave."

"Hannah," Liberty huffed out a breath. "I told you, it's not true. There is no magical cave."

Hannah tugged out of Liberty's grip and wiped tears from her cheeks. "But what if there is? What if I could save my grandpa and I didn't even try? What if he dies?" Her voice rose in hysteria.

"Okay, okay. I'm sorry. Just calm down. If you promise not to go off on your own again, I'll help you find the cave."

"You will?" Hannah's watery eyes lit with hope.

"Yes, but you have to promise me—"

A flapping sound drew Liberty's attention. She whirled to find a huge bat soaring directly toward her. She squealed and grabbed Hannah, dropping to the ground with her body shielding the girl.

When nothing happened, Liberty peeked from between her arms and saw the bat hovering above them.

It was a vampire, it had to be. She assumed all bats on the island were vampires. But who? Friend or foe? A friend likely wouldn't terrify them like that. She suffered a moment of embarrassment. Her actions hadn't exactly been that of a hunter, but in spite of all she'd seen and done, bats still freaked her out.

But she couldn't keep cowering in fear. She rose and rushed at the bat, waving her arms. It flew back a ways, then soared toward her.

Liberty's insides quaked with fear. Crazy that she was more frightened of them in their bat form than vampire form.

The bat hovered in the air. A squeaking, screeching sound filled the night and the bat began to change shape. Liberty shuddered with revulsion as the beast's pointed face morphed in front of her eyes into a man's face. Its body stretched into a man's torso, the wings became arms and legs.

"Oh my God," Hannah screeched. "What's happening? Oh my God… what is that?"

Great. Eli wasn't here to mesmerize Hannah this time. Liberty couldn't worry about that now.

She recognized the vampire immediately. Trey. He'd confronted her the night of the hunt, threatened to capture her for Rupert while claiming he wanted her for his own. He was a freak—and scary as hell.

He whirled and stalked toward Liberty. "Well, well, if it isn't Miss Liberty Van Helsing and a little golden ball of human sunshine. No full moon tonight. Pity. I'm just aching to turn someone."

"Yeah. Pity." Liberty backed away, reaching into the compression holster at her back for the pistol she now carried constantly—a pistol loaded with wooden bullets. She hadn't had to use it, but it would have come in handy the night of the festival. And the likelihood was certainly pointing that direction now. A thought struck icy fear in her chest. Was Trey the killer?

If so, it was bad news and good news. Bad news, he was even more demented than she thought. Good news, she could end this here and now.

He executed an odd, head cocking thing, like a chicken studying a kernel of corn. Slowly, he advanced. From the corner of her eye, Liberty saw Hannah rise to her feet. Her entire body trembled. Her face was pale, her eyes round in shock.

Please run. Don't do anything stupid… just go!

Liberty tried to keep her attention on Trey while at the same time eyeing Hannah. Hoping she would be smart.

"What do you want?" Liberty demanded. "Rupert has called off his orders to capture me until the rogue vampire is caught. We have a truce."

He laughed, a sound like demons cackling. "*He* has a truce. I made no such deal."

"But he's your leader. You have to obey him. He'll make you pay if you don't."

He shrugged. "Some things are worth the risk."

She aimed the gun at his heart. "This is a risk I don't think you want to take."

His eyes flickered momentarily with… fear… insane delight?

"Oh, my precious. I'll be the judge of that."

He lunged, and she pulled the trigger. The bullet hit his shoulder, spun him around, and he dropped to the dirt. But he was barely injured. He rose to his feet. She took more careful aim but before she could pull the trigger, Hannah jumped him from behind. She'd somehow found a piece of wood and plunged it into him. Blood leaked from his shoulder and his back. He growled like a furious, wounded animal, but didn't go down and smolder into a pile of ashes. They'd both missed his heart.

He staggered toward Hannah. She backed up, shaking her head, "Please, please don't hurt me."

Terror froze Liberty's insides. Hannah's life was in danger because Liberty had refused to help her when the girl asked… and because Hannah had attempted to protect Liberty. If something happened to her…

Just as Trey reached Hannah, yanked her to him, and pulled her head back, exposing her neck, Liberty pulled the trigger and let out another volley of shots. Trey's body spasmed and jerked. Hannah fell to the ground.

Chapter 10

Trey swayed drunkenly toward Liberty. Damn. She'd missed his heart again. She took aim again and pulled the trigger. Got nothing but a hollow click. Trey seemed not to notice. Although still standing, he had to be in some pretty righteous pain.

He blinked twice and peered at her through reddened eyes. "I'll be back, Liberty. You'll never be free of me."

He whirled and lurched away, into the darkness.

Liberty's entire body went limp. She dropped the gun. "Hannah, he's gone. Are you okay?"

Hannah didn't respond. Liberty looked to where she lay—deathly still. Blood pooled at her head.

"Oh my God." Liberty knelt next to her and put a hand on her wrist to check her pulse. Thready, but at least she had a pulse. Her breathing was shallow. When Trey had thrown her, she'd taken a hard hit. So much blood… she was dying.

Liberty closed her mind to the nauseating river of red. She fumbled in her pockets for the vial, breathing a sigh of relief when her fingers gripped the glass.

She removed the cap and gently opened Hannah's mouth, placing the vial between her lips. Liberty tried not to think about what she was doing—the fact that she was not only this close to blood, but she was actually feeding it to someone. She swallowed back a lump of bile.

"Drink this, sweetie. Come on, drink it. Swallow for me. You'll be fine. I promise." Liberty held back tears, praying this would work. If Hannah died because of her—if she died at all—Liberty would never forgive herself.

Hannah's throat moved, and Liberty let out a sigh of relief. She was drinking.

Hannah moaned and lifted her eyelids. She looked up at Liberty, but her gaze didn't seem quite focused. "Was that—was he a—vampire?"

"A vampire? That's crazy."

"It's crazy, but I know what I saw."

Hannah sat up and looked around, her eyes wide. "Where is he? *What* is he?" Her hand went back to touch the blood on her head. She frowned. "Nothing hurts, but that's a lot of blood."

"Uhm… well, it's not your blood." The implausible lie fell from Liberty's lips. "The guy who attacked you was injured, you stumbled and fell back into his blood."

Hannah's frown deepened. "That seems… impossible. I saw a bat—I saw him change…" She shook her head. "How can that be?"

Liberty smoothed the blonde hair back from Hannah's face. "It can't be, sweetie. You hit your head pretty hard. You imagined all that. He was just some crazy guy, probably on drugs. He's gone now."

"I don't know…"

"Let's get you home. You'll feel better after a night's rest."

Hannah nodded uncertainly, and Liberty helped her to her feet. She didn't know how long the girl would fall for the story. Maybe she'd have to ask Eli—or someone—to mesmerize her again. But how long could they really keep the secret from the girl? Two instances thus far. Maybe Hannah should learn the truth for her own safety.

But not tonight. Tonight, Liberty had to think back over what had happened, try to figure out if Trey was the killer. She had a feeling he wasn't. Just a gut feeling, but it was a strong one.

Regardless whether Trey was the one they were hunting, the vampire who preyed on young girls was still out there. Free to murder again.

****

Antoine's face was drawn into a scowl as he wrapped the tourniquet around Liberty's upper arm. "You must exercise caution in using the vials of blood." He held up the syringe, waiting for her to turn her head before he plunged the needle into her vein. "I cannot continue to take your blood on a regular basis. It will make you weak."

She squeezed her eyes shut when the needle pricked her flesh. She didn't mind the pain, but the thought of what was happening, that her blood was flowing out of her veins gave her heart palpitations.

"What am I supposed to do when someone is in danger?" she asked through gritted teeth. "When they need my help?"

He chuckled. "That is what hospitals are for, my child. You should only use your blood in extreme life and death situations. When it is the only way."

"I was pretty sure with Hannah it was the only way." She paused. "Relatively sure. How can I know?"

"That is not an easy question to answer. You must learn to know. That is all." She felt him wrap a bandage around her elbow and the bend of her arm. "You can open your eyes now."

She did, cautiously turning her head. The vials were sealed. He'd purchased colored, opaque glass so she didn't have to actually look at the blood unless it was absolutely necessary. Although Antoine was reserved, formal, his thoughtfulness showed he was growing fond of her. He'd been with her father for over twenty years, and had cared deeply for him.

"Now perhaps you should go get some rest." Antoine took her hand and helped her from the chair.

"I don't think I can." She was bruised and battered, sad, restless. Her mind wouldn't compute all she'd learned from Rupert, on top of the run-in with Trey.

She hated that she couldn't know without a doubt whether Trey was the killer. But the vampire was targeting young innocent girls. Trey was there for his single minded purpose of—what? Capturing her for Rupert? For himself? Or just screwing with her because he was a nut job?

"Would you like some warm milk?"

She smiled. "No, thank you. I think I'll go to the cemetery."

Sadness touched his Polynesian features. He inclined his head. "As you wish. Would you like some company?"

"I think I'd like to visit him alone."

"Very well. Be careful, Miss."

"Of course."

She drove to the graveyard and slowly cruised down the narrow paths until she reached the row where Victor was buried.

The headstones loomed in the darkness, her way

barely lit by the moon shining through the trees.

She found her father's grave and knelt beside it, rubbed a hand along his stone.

"I wish you were here, Dad. That it wasn't all on me to find my way. I wasn't ready to be a hunter yet." A sob caught in her chest. Tears formed in her eyes, and she wiped them with the back of her hand. "I would have loved to learn it all from you instead of freakin' Eli."

But her encounter with Trey made her realize, in spite of how much she didn't want to, she definitely needed to train with Eli. She should have nailed Trey's heart with the first shot. She'd missed every single shot.

"I know it's foolish, useless to wish for things than can never be, but I also wish Mom remembered you. Remembered our time here. I bet she loved you and never would have left if you hadn't erased her memory. You cheated us both." He'd done it to protect them, but it still ate at her. How different would her life be if she'd been raised here on the island, as a Van Helsing with a loving mother and father? Her mom was great, but growing up without a father had been no picnic.

"He didn't erase her memory. I did."

She jumped to her feet and whirled. A man headed toward her from the shadows of the trees. Her heart raced with fear. He stepped closer. He wore a gray suit jacket and a fedora covered most of his dark hair. The bright pink handkerchief jutting from this suit jacket pocket should have looked incongruous, but it made him look... dashing. He was medium height, fit, handsome. Looked to be in his early forties. But if he was a vampire, and she was guessing he was, he could be hundreds of years old.

She swallowed, the dryness in her throat clicking loudly in the silence. "Who—who are you?"

"I'm Paul Blackwell." He extended a hand, but when she didn't take it, he let his drop. "I'm an old friend of your father's." He gave a wistful smile. "And of your mother's. At least at one time. She no longer remembers me."

"You're the one who mesmerized her?"

He nodded. "I did so at your father's request. I advised him against it. I told him that you and your mother would rather know him, stay with him, in spite of the dangers, than to lose all trace of memory of him."

"But you did it anyway."

"Yes. I'm afraid so. Your father wouldn't listen. I was his best friend. I had to do as he asked. Even if I thought him a fool."

Although she wasn't sure she could trust this man, she was hungry for information on her past. "What were they like? My parents? What were we like as a family?"

He smiled. "Happy. Very happy. Your mother was… breathtakingly beautiful, kind, funny…" He blinked rapidly and even in the darkness, she saw a faint tinge of red rise to his face.

She didn't ask if he loved her mother, but she knew he had. She could see it in his expression. Hear it in his voice when he spoke of her. Had her mother known? Had her father? Paul Blackwell had been Victor's best friend. Maybe he hadn't acted on his feelings. She wanted to believe that, anyway.

"Then came that awful day," he said. "The day at the ice cream store." She was surprised to see tears glisten in his eyes. "Everything changed that day. Your father was like a man possessed, determined to do whatever it took to protect you both. He practically went to pieces at how close he'd come to losing you." He stared at her intently.

"I'll admit, I'd never seen such a horrifying sight. A small, fragile little girl, drenched in blood. If Eli hadn't—" He halted, his gaze dropping away.

"If Eli hadn't what?" she prompted.

"Nothing. It's not important."

She stalked up to him and tilted her head back to stare into his face. His eyes were a light brown, almost golden. He was extremely good-looking. For an older guy. If her mother knew of his feelings, Liberty could see how she might be tempted. "What are you talking about? What does Eli have to do with this?" She crossed her arms, stopping short of stomping her foot like a child. "I have a right to know."

He gave a slight nod. "Yes, yes you do. But you'll have to get your answers from Eli."

"Why is that? You told me so many other things."

"Yes, but this is Eli's thing to tell you. I have too much respect for him to betray him."

"Respect? Up until a year ago, wasn't he one of the vicious, psycho vampires running amok?"

He chuckled. "Running amok? I like that. To answer your question, yes, he was. But even malevolent hearts can sometimes show a flicker of compassion, of heroism. Even the non-beating ones."

"And I suppose Eli did something heroic? That's why you respect him? Was it in the ice cream shop?" Her knees weakened at the realization that Eli might have been there during the bloodbath. Kind of creepy, really, that he was a grown man when she was three. Technically, though, he had been twenty-one, just like he was now. And she was eighteen. Not so creepy at all. "Did he save us?"

He stuck out his hand again, and she took it this

time. "It was lovely chatting with you, Liberty. You've grown into a beautiful young woman. I can see both your mother and your father in you."

She shook his hand, disappointment curling in her stomach. "You're not going to tell me, are you?"

He winked and tipped his hat. "Talk to Eli."

Chapter 11

Liberty walked silently beside Eli. They'd been in town for hours, and hadn't seen a hint of the vampire they were looking for. Eli had discreetly mesmerized some of the customers at a few bars, hoping to find out if they'd seen anything useful the night the first victim was taken, but his efforts hadn't paid off.

All through the evening, Liberty had been waiting for the right time to ask Eli about the ice cream shop. Or, more accurately, to work up the nerve to ask. She knew he wouldn't be forthcoming, so she'd held off. She wasn't sure she was ready to beg, or ready for the disappointment when he refused to tell her.

"You know," she said. "Maybe we're going about this all wrong. We should be a little more discreet, crafty. Maybe we should bait this guy."

"Bait him how?" Eli shoved his hands in his pockets and flicked a glance at her.

"We know he goes for young girls, partying usually. And that they are either alone or with one other person."

"You're talking about using some young, innocent girls to entice him?" He grinned. "I like that idea."

She frowned. "No, not exactly. I'm not as willing to risk the innocent as you are. I was thinking I could lure him in. The problem is, this guy most likely knows who I am. Maybe I could wear a disguise—"

A scream tore through the night, cutting her off.

Twenty feet ahead, two figures struggled on the sidewalk. Liberty took off at a run. Eli zipped past her and was pulling a man off of a young woman when she arrived. Blood poured from the woman's neck.

"Oh my God." Liberty drew in a labored breath, winded from her sprint. She rushed to the girl and checked the wound on her neck. The blood made Liberty's stomach clench, but she pushed back the nausea. "Are you okay?" The bite hadn't bled all that much and didn't look deep. They'd gotten to her in time.

"I—I can't believe…" The girl was plump, with brown hair and pretty features. Her eyes were as round as dinner plates. "He… he just attacked me."

Liberty turned to see that Eli had the vampire in a headlock. The vampire narrowed his eyes at Liberty and grinned with his blood-smeared mouth.

"You need to do this," Eli said to her. "I could, but it's your job. Take him out so his line will ultimately die off."

"I don't… don't know if…"

"Do it," Eli demanded. "Draw your weapon and end him."

She hesitated. It was one thing to fire at a vampire attacking someone. Another entirely to shoot one while he was pinned down, helpless.

With a shaking hand, she pulled the gun from her waistband and held it on the vampire. She bit her lip and shook her head. "I—I can't."

"Don't hurt him," the woman cried out weakly.

Liberty frowned in puzzlement. Why would the vampire's victim not want him harmed? Had he mesmerized her?

"You have to," Eli ground out.

Liberty drew in a breath. "But he's—you have him captured. We can just take him in. I can't kill someone who can't fight back."

Eli's mouth turned up at the corner. "No? Maybe this will help."

He shoved the vampire toward her. A furious snarl tore from the vampire's throat, and he rushed her. Liberty gasped, firing off three shots in succession. She must have improved her aim, because the vampire dropped in a heap at her feet.

Behind Liberty, the woman let out an agonized sob. Liberty barely noticed. Now that the adrenaline rush was over, rage set in. She whirled on Eli. "You—you let him go! He could have killed me."

Eli shrugged. "Yeah but he didn't."

"Huh! You're unbelievable." She shook her head, blinking back tears of fury.

Her eyes went back down to the body. She blinked rapidly, her mind trying to compute what she was seeing—rather, what she was *not* seeing. She lifted her gaze to Eli. He stared at her, his eyes squinted.

"He's not smoldering into ashes," she whispered.

Eli grimaced. "He is not."

"Oh my God. I murdered a human."

"He was trying to hurt the girl."

The woman staggered to where the man lay and dropped to her knees beside him. She sobbed brokenly. "No, he wouldn't have," she screamed. "He wouldn't hurt me. He loves me." Another sob tore from her throat. "We were going to be married. Tomorrow."

"But—your-your neck," Liberty stammered. "He attacked you. Bit your neck. He was going to…" What? Why would a human feed on another human? How was he able to tear into her flesh like that without fangs? He must have been determined—insane?

The woman shook her head, holding onto her fiancé's hand and weeping. "I don't know. I don't know what came over him. We were out. Having a good time. Talking to some people. We left this bar, and suddenly, he started acting strangely, he had this weird look in his eyes. He turned on me, bit my neck. Yes, he was hurting me, but I could have gotten through to him. Could have stopped him." She rose to her feet and spun on Liberty. "But you killed him!" She formed her hands into claws and lunged.

Eli moved in a flash and gripped the woman's neck in his hand.

"Eli, no!" Liberty shouted.

He didn't stop. Didn't flinch. The woman's face was turning red, she scrabbled at his hold.

"Eli!" Liberty rushed to him, tugged on his arm. "Let her go. You'll kill her."

His hand relaxed slightly. The woman gasped for air. He didn't let go.

"Look at me," he commanded.

She lifted her eyes to his.

"I want you to focus and listen to me."

She nodded.

"Who was your fiancé talking to earlier tonight?"

She shook her head. The tears had stopped flowing. "People… a few people."

"There was someone, probably a man, most likely the last person he spoke with before he started acting… strange."

She nodded again. "But I don't know his name."

"What did he look like?"

She seemed to concentrate for a few moments. "He was nice-looking. Dark hair. Sort of tall. Blue eyes."

"Was there anything unique about him? Scars? Tattoos? The clothes he wore?"

"I remember... he had a-a pink handkerchief in his suit pocket."

Liberty drew in a sharp breath, and Eli turned to her. "That means something to you?"

"Yes. A man at the cemetery. When I went to visit my father's grave."

"What man?"

"He wasn't really a..." She shot a look at the woman. "...a man, if you know what I mean."

"Yeah, I know what you mean. Who was he?"

"Paul Blackwell. He said he was a friend of my father's."

Eli's eyes narrowed. "I know him. He can't be the one. He doesn't have it in him."

"Maybe you don't know him as well as you thought you did."

Eli let out a heavy sigh. "Maybe I don't. I'll check him out, but I'm sure it's a dead end." He turned back to the woman and captured her gaze. "You'll forget everything that happened here. Your fiancé was shot by an unknown assailant. You didn't see anything."

She nodded. "I didn't see anything."

He released her and she backed away, a hand on her throat. Blood had started leaking again. He pulled his cell out and dialed. "Operator? We need an ambulance at the Tropicana. A man is dead, and a woman's been badly injured."

"Help is on its way," he told the woman when he hung up. He took Liberty's arm. "Let's get out of here."

She walked with him, her body shaking. "I—can't believe I..." She sniffed back tears and shuddered.

Eli pulled her against his side, wrapped his arm tightly around her and rubbed his hand up and down her arm. Although his flesh was cold, each time he touched her she experienced an odd warmth. She couldn't make sense of it. But right now, she couldn't make sense of anything. She'd just taken a human life. The life of an innocent—well basically innocent—man.

"What was that all about?" Liberty shook her head, still not believing what had just happened. "Why would a human attack his fiancée like that?"

Eli released a sigh. "I have a feeling our guy might have mesmerized him. She said he was talking to someone. Maybe it was the killer."

"This guy is sick. Beyond sick." She pulled away. "You shouldn't have mesmerized her. She might have answers for us. More than just the ones she gave."

"Even if she did, we wouldn't know if they were accurate. The bastard could have mesmerized her to say anything to get us off his trail."

"So she could have been wrong about Paul. Now that I think about it, Paul's eyes are brownish-gold, not blue." She scraped a hand through her hair. "God, who could be doing this?" She looked up at him. "I should tell the police what happened. It's the right thing to do. You can't just mesmerize all my problems away."

"No, if I could do that, I would mesmerize you to forget this place and go back to Oklahoma like a good little girl."

"You still want me off the island."

He stared into her eyes, his holding a glint of moonlight. He brushed her hair back from her face.

"What I want is for you to be safe."

She compressed her lips. "Don't."

"Don't what?"

"Don't act like you care one minute, then be an asshole the next."

He gave a humorless laugh. "Stick with the asshole routine, then?"

"It suits you better."

He flinched almost imperceptibly and stepped away from her. "I suppose it does at that. I'll pick you up tomorrow night. Maybe we can work on finding the murdering vampire instead of slaying humans."

She sucked in a sharp breath and fought back tears. She'd asked for it. He was being an asshole just like she'd requested. She had no one to blame but herself. And, the truly awful part was, he was right.

****

Liberty lay in bed, the comforter pulled over her head. She'd been there all day. Had called into work. Since last night, she hadn't been able to think of anything other than the fact that she'd taken a human life. How could she have done something so terrible? It didn't matter that she'd thought he was a vampire, that he was hurting the woman. Her instincts should have warned her that he was just a man. What kind of self-respecting hunter couldn't recognize a vampire when she saw one?

She sniffed back tears and rolled over on her side.

Her door opened, but she didn't remove the covers. "Go away, Antoine." He'd been to her room half a dozen times trying to coax her out of bed, trying to feed her. She knew he meant well but she just wanted to be left alone.

"It's not Antoine."

Before she could react to hearing Eli's voice, the covers were yanked away. She sat up and tried to snatch them back, but Eli held them from her.

"What the hell do you think you're doing?" she demanded. "Get out."

He shook his head, grinning smugly. "Nope. Not gonna happen. You're going to have to get over it. Like, now."

She infused her voice with sarcasm. "I'm afraid I can't take killing in stride like you can."

He lifted his brows. "Don't apologize. It's nothing to be embarrassed about."

"Oh God you're annoying," she groaned and brought her knees up and dropped her face into her hands. "Would you please just go?"

"Get dressed. We have work to do. The captain called, and it wasn't to congratulate us on the fine job we're doing. They want results."

She lifted her chin and glowered at him. "You do know we don't work for the captain, right?"

"You do know we need to stop this guy, right? I looked for Blackwell, but couldn't find him. We're no closer than we were in the beginning. Not even a millimeter closer." He rummaged through her closet and yanked a shirt and a skirt off hangers. He flung them at her. "Get dressed."

She held one garment in each hand. "These don't even match."

"Then find something to put on, or I'll dress you myself." He strode to the door. "You have five minutes."

"Asshole," she muttered after he'd gone.

She took a quick shower and pulled on jeans and a Rock Louie t-shirt. She went downstairs where Eli waited in the foyer with Antoine.

"I see Eli was more successful than I." Antoine smiled in satisfaction.

"Yes, but he used caveman tactics." She shot Eli a look that was meant to be quelling.

He wasn't fazed. "Ready?" he asked.

"I suppose." She stomped past him and headed outside. "Where to?" she bit out when he joined her on the porch.

"Boardwalk. That's where the tourists hang. Maybe we'll get lucky tonight."

She blew a breath up and ruffled her bangs. "I still think we should run a check on the vampires who have been turned recently."

"And how do you propose we do that? I told you, they're not exactly entered into a database."

"We could question vampires, from both sides. They could introduce us to their recent…"

"Apprentices."

"Yeah, apprentices."

He crooked a grin. "Interview with a Vampire, huh?"

She smiled in spite of her foul mood. "Something like that."

"Might not be a bad idea. In the meantime, let's go hang at the boardwalk. I'll drive."

Chapter 12

Three hours of pretending to be tourists, and nothing—not a sign or clue of anything out of the ordinary.

Liberty dropped wearily onto a bench in front of a Starbuck's. She drew in a deep breath, enjoying the smell of fresh ground coffee beans mixed with the ocean air. From somewhere down the boardwalk, the distant strains of "Can't Help Falling in Love" by Elvis Presley filtered to her.

She bit her lip and studied Eli from beneath her lashes. Paul's words had been weighing on her mind for days, and now she was going to get an answer—or at least attempt to. "Eli, can I ask you something?"

"It's a free country." He dropped to the bench beside her.

"Were you there?" She swallowed. "Were you in the ice cream shop when I was a child? During the attack?"

He frowned. "Why would you ask me that?"

"Just something I heard. Tell me."

He blew a breath out between his lips. "Yeah. I was there."

"But you weren't one of the vampires who attacked us."

"No."

"You helped us."

He shrugged. "I might have."

"No, you did. Back then you were one of the Evil Ones. Why did you help?"

"It was a long time ago. It's not important."

She rested a hand on his forearm. He looked at it, then up at her eyes. "It's important to me."

He stared at her silently for so long, she thought he wasn't going to tell her. Finally, he said, "Even as bad as I was, I couldn't stand by and watch a child being…" He scrubbed his hands over his face. "…well, you know. And even the others… I saw the happy smiles. I remembered for just a moment what it was like to be human." His jaw clenched. "You and your dad were next. As Van Helsings, you were the targets."

"And you could have rid the island of Van Helsings by just standing back and doing nothing."

He chuckled. "Yeah, what was I thinking, right?"

"Is that why my father befriended you?"

"That was years later."

"Yes, but he must have remembered you from that day. Tell me how it all happened."

He tightened his jaw. "We don't really need to talk about this. We have other matters to deal with."

"Let me ask you one more thing." She didn't know why she was pushing, why she wanted to know, but she felt the need to dig into his soul, to see what went on behind those enchanting light grey eyes. To know what he really felt about her. Once and for all. She and Ryan were close to a commitment, but she needed to deal with her feelings for Eli. One minute she hated him, the next she craved his touch. Beneath it all was the constant yearning. The need for… something…

"So, ask."

"When we first met, you tried to mesmerize me into

kissing you. Was that just a ploy you use on all women you meet? Some kind of game?"

"More or less." He wouldn't meet her eyes. He laughed. "Little did I know I didn't have to use any tricks. You were easy."

That stung, but she wouldn't let his shield of sarcasm reroute her from her goal. "Is that really all it was? A game? What about all the flirting? The times I see... something... in your eyes. Do you have feelings for me?" There. She'd said it. She'd never been that brazen, but somehow the need to know gave her bravado.

Now he turned to her. His brows were drawn over his eyes, his expression thunderous. "Don't ask questions you don't want the answers to."

"But I do. I want to know. How do you feel about me?"

His gaze moved over her face, paused at her mouth, then rose to her eyes. "How I feel doesn't matter. We can never be together."

"Why not?" She couldn't believe she said the words even as they fell from her lips. She cared about Ryan. A lot. The last thing she needed was a brooding, dangerous vampire. But still, she waited breathlessly for his answer.

"You mean other than the age difference?"

"Age difference?"

"Sure. You're eighteen and I'm three-hundred."

She rolled her eyes. "Can you please be serious? Just give me a straight answer."

He looked out over the ocean as he spoke. "You are the last of the Van Helsings. It's your duty to carry on the lineage. That means children. Something I can never give you. Something that Ryan can. He loves you. You need to be with him."

Her mouth dropped open and she pushed to her feet, scraping her hair back from her forehead. *Children*? It was up to her to carry on the Van Helsing bloodline, or the human race would suffer. For God's sake, that was a heavy burden to bear.

He stood also and took hold of her upper arms, pulled her closer. "Now let me ask you something. Would it make a difference if we could be together? Are you in love with Ryan?" His voice lowered. "Or do you have feelings for me?"

She opened her mouth, but nothing came out. How could she admit to him what she didn't know herself?

Finally, she managed to speak. "I—I, I don't know what—"

"There you are." Ryan's voice broke the moment and Eli released her abruptly and stepped back.

She turned a smile on Ryan, hoping to hide her inner turmoil. "Hey. What are you doing here?"

He slung an arm around her shoulder, gave her a peck on the cheek. "I've missed you." He looked at Eli. "I was hoping I could steal you away for a while. I think you need a break."

"What did you have in mind?"

He pulled her into his arms, cupped his hands on the back of her head and kissed her. "You'll see," he whispered.

She glanced at Eli from the corners of her eyes. His mouth was tight, his eyes glittering. Jealous? Or just pissed in general? Not that it mattered, as he'd made clear, the two of them could never be together. He had just been toying with her.

Some childish need for retaliation made her wrap her arms around Ryan's neck and return the kiss, passionately, thoroughly. "I can't wait to find out."

****

Eli sat on a bar stool at the Blind Lady, an out of the way, all-nighter dive on the outskirts of town. He lifted the glass to his lips and drained it, then slid it back to the bartender.

"Another? This makes your third," Malcolm said.

"Keep them coming until I tell you to stop."

"Is it the girl?"

Eli grunted a bitter laugh. "Isn't it always?"

Malcolm slid him another scotch and Eli lifted it to his lips.

"You've got it bad for her," Malcolm leaned forward and crossed his arms on the bar.

Eli nodded. "It's tough. Being around her. Knowing I can't have her."

Malcolm nodded. "Life's like that sometimes."

"Yeah, yeah it is." Eli tipped his glass toward the bartender. "Thanks for listening, brother. You're the only one I can talk to about it."

"Any time. No other customers right now. Want to tell me what happened?"

Eli sighed and finished his drink. Malcolm rose and poured another.

"Every time I'm around her, it's like this weird kind of exquisite torture. When I'm not, it's even worse. I think about her day and night. I crave her like I've never craved blood."

Malcolm whistled. "Man. I've never felt that way about a woman."

"I haven't either. I've loved women, don't get me wrong. In the hundreds of years I've been alive, I've loved lots of women. But never like this." A stone of pain settled in his chest. "Sometimes when I look at her, I can't breathe." He choked out a laugh and shook his head. "I loved Christelle, but not like I love Liberty. She… consumes me. Being with Christelle made me happy. With Liberty, I want to make *her* happy."

"Damn." Malcolm shook his head in sympathy.

"Tell me about it." Eli took another hit off his scotch. "There are times, like when I saw her and Ryan kissing, I get this explosion in my brain, this red curtain falls over everything and I don't think, I just react. That's why I did what I did."

"What did you do?"

Eli shook his head and smiled. "Talk's over buddy. Now, look at me. Focus."

Malcolm stared into Eli's eyes.

"You won't remember a word of our conversation, you understand?" Eli said.

The bartender nodded.

"Good." Eli drained his glass, still holding Malcolm's gaze. "Remember, I was never here."

Chapter 13

Liberty whistled—literally whistled, how lame was that?—as she drove to work. She was still on a cloud from last night's date. It had been the best time of her life. She and Ryan had a late dinner on the beach and, afterward, lay on the blanket watching the stars glint like diamonds in the black sky.

Ryan had been romantic, the night magical, and after an hour or so, she barely thought about Eli. He wasn't the man for her. In many ways. And now that she knew it was her responsibility to continue the Van Helsing line, that pretty much sealed it. Ryan was the one she should be with.

Not that she was ready to have babies with him—or anyone for that matter—but he was definitely worth pursuing a relationship with. He loved her, not only had he told her, but she could see it in his eyes. She cared about him a lot, but was it love? Maybe not yet, but it could be. She thought back to his warm kisses last night that sent electricity zinging to her toes. Yes, it definitely could be.

She parked at the Perfect Getaway, climbed out of her car and headed in. Tonight, she didn't even mind working. She actually looked forward to it. Ryan would be there.

She spotted him at his usual post as soon as she walked in. He wore a tight black t-shirt and jeans. His dark hair flipped over his forehead, making her fingers itch to brush it back.

She walked over to the bar and leaned against it, giving him a smile. "Hey there,"

He glanced back at her. "Yeah? What's up?" He poured a vodka soda.

"Uh, just wanted to say hi."

"Well, you said it." He glanced at her, then back to the drink he was making. "I'm kind of busy here, and don't you need to start your shift?"

She frowned, confusion warring with hurt. "What's wrong?"

"What do you mean, wrong?"

"You seem... cold. Did something happen?" Had he thought about coming up on her and Eli last night and decided there was more to it than he'd first thought? He hadn't questioned her about it last night, hadn't said a word.

He looked at her and gave a weary sigh. "Nothing happened, okay? I have work to do. And so do you."

She reached out and grabbed his hand where it rested on the bar. "Ryan, look at me. I know there's something wrong. You seem... upset with me."

He pulled his hand away. "Not upset. Not... anything. At all."

"What do you mean not anything at all?"

He narrowed his eyes and shook his head. "I can't explain it. Yesterday, I thought my world revolved around you. I loved you more than I've ever loved anyone." He laughed. Shrugged. "Today, it's all changed. You mean nothing to me."

She gasped and stepped back. Pain shafted through her heart and tears filled her eyes. "You don't mean that," she choked out.

He laughed again. "As crazy as it sounds, I actually do. I guess you were nothing more than a summer fling. Who knew, right?"

****

Melody walked down the sidewalk, digging in her purse for her cell. Her parents were going to kill her. Literally. They'd brought her to the island for her eighteenth birthday but expected her to spend all her time with them. What kind of birthday was that? She'd snuck out earlier, planning on partying for just a few hours. Now she was hammered. And had no idea how to get back to the hotel. She hadn't seen a cab. She had no choice but to call her parents.

She fished out her phone and was dialing her mother's number when footsteps sounded behind her.

Fear pierced her chest. She swallowed, not wanting to turn around, but afraid not to. Slowly, she glanced over her shoulder. A figure stood in the shadows. She couldn't make out any features, but it was a man, she was sure about that.

"Hello?" she said shakily. "Can I help you?"

Her fingers continued to tap the numbers but before she could push 'send,' he was on her, snatching the cell from her grip.

"You won't need that," he said. He gripped her shoulders. "Look at me. Look into my eyes and listen carefully to what I say."

She looked into his eyes—the most beautiful eyes she'd ever seen. "Please… please don't hurt me."

His mouth twisted in an evil smile. "Well, I can assure you I'm not going to *kill* you. I have other plans. I want you to describe me to the police. Tell them I had dark blond hair, grey eyes, and my name is Eli."

She felt funny. Like she was in some kind of trance. Was it the alcohol? She slowly nodded. "Your name is Eli."

"Now, brace yourself. I'm going to make this a very bad night for you."

His head dipped, and his mouth latched onto her neck. It felt like sharp, thick needles were biting into her flesh. Something wet—blood she realized—trickled down her neck. Agony ripped through her throat, into her chest. She couldn't scream. Couldn't speak, couldn't breathe. She grew weaker, feeling the life drain from her limbs as he drank. Drank her blood... dear God, what was happening?

Blackness swam in her vision. The ground rushed up to meet her as he released her shoulders. She hit the cement with a bone jarring thud. Something was pressed into her hand. A piece of paper...? That was the last thing she remembered before the darkness took her. That and the name... Eli...

****

The night moved in slow agony for Liberty. Her heart was breaking. Much worse than when Cam cheated. Did that mean she loved Ryan? What could have changed his mind so abruptly? Was he really just a player and she hadn't seen it?

She dug into her pocket and pulled out the coin he'd given her—to help 'ground' her, he'd said. To give her something to hold onto so she wouldn't be afraid. He told her a story about how his father had given him one just like it when he was a child, one that helped him when he was frightened. But Bianca had told Liberty the coin wasn't just like the one his father had given him. It was *the* coin. And that had been when he'd just met her. Why would he do that if he was now able to toss her aside so easily?

She drew in a deep breath. No sense dwelling on it. Whatever they had was over. Ryan no longer wanted her. He'd made that clear.

Her phone rang as she was heading to the parking lot after her shift.

It was the captain. "I need you to get to the hospital right away."

"What is it?" Her heart thudded heavily in her chest.

"Another victim. Though this one is alive. She's talking. Rupert and Blake are here."

"What about Eli? I'll call him and—"

"No," he cut her off sharply. "Don't call Eli. Just get here and I'll explain."

She sped to the hospital, her already muddled mind trying to make sense of the cryptic phone call. Why not call Eli? Explain what?

She parked in the emergency parking lot and rushed through the doors. The captain was in the waiting room with Rupert and Blake.

"Follow me." The captain didn't wait for her to agree. He headed down the hallway. She, Rupert, and Blake followed.

They entered a room where a young blonde girl lay with bandages around her neck and head. Her eyes were closed, her face pale. Blue shadows veined her lids and beneath her eyes.

"Melody?" The captain's tone was gentle. "Are you awake? Do you feel like talking?"

The girl's eyes slowly opened. Fear hovered in their hazel depths.

"This is Liberty Van Helsing. I'm going to tell her what happened. You don't have to talk any more. You can just confirm what I say is accurate."

She gave a slight nod.

"You were attacked this evening by a man. Tall, grey eyes, dark blond hair."

Another nod.

"He gave you this." The captain held up a piece of paper with an oak tree drawing. "And he told you his name was Eli."

Liberty drew in a sharp breath. Eli? Not possible. But the girl nodded.

The captain turned to Liberty. "All this time he's pretending to help. And it turns out he's our killer."

"No." She shook her head. "No way. He wouldn't do that. And if he did, he damn sure wouldn't tell her his name."

"Maybe he gets some perverse thrill out of them knowing who he is. Maybe he makes them call him by name. I'm sure he didn't expect her to live. It's a miracle she did. Her throat was nearly torn out."

Bile rose in Liberty's chest at the thought of Eli savagely attacking this fragile young girl. It couldn't be. "No," she whispered.

"There's more," Blake said.

The captain shot him a look. "Yes, there's more. Let's step into the hall."

They left the girl's room. Liberty's legs were so weak, they could barely carry her. First Ryan, now Eli? She couldn't accept that these two men—men she thought she knew—could be capable of something like this. Especially Eli. Brutally murdering young girls was so much worse than breaking her heart.

She crossed her arms and looked up at the captain. "What? What's this 'more'?"

Blake spoke for the captain. "In the revolutionary war, Eli was a prisoner. He was locked up in Connecticut for two years. This tree stood just outside his window." He pointed to the paper the captain held.

"This tree?" She gave an incredulous laugh. "It's an oak tree. Like billions of other oak trees."

"No, no it isn't at all." He gritted his jaw and met her gaze. "It's a Charter Oak. The symbol for freedom. The Connecticut state symbol. I don't know why I didn't recognize it initially, but after the girl told us Eli attacked her, it all clicked in place."

She shook her head. "But why? Why would he do that? It would make him an enemy of both camps. Not to mention, he's not that… evil."

"You didn't know him before," the captain said. "He's changed in the last year." He gave a humorless laugh. "But maybe not as much as we thought."

"Yes." Rupert sighed heavily, speaking for the first time. "Maybe he felt he didn't really belong in either world." His face was drawn and he seemed to have aged ten years, even though a vampire couldn't age. Why would he be so disturbed to find out Eli was the killer—the traitor? She'd seen glimpses of mild admiration from him toward Eli, but this went deeper than that.

Her mind rebelled against the indisputable evidence. But maybe he was right about Eli. Maybe they all were. "Does Eli know about any of this?"

The captain shook his head. "We weren't sure how to approach him. You need to be the one to take him down."

Takes him down… kill Eli?

Tears rose to her throat, but she didn't let them fall.

"I can send my men with you," Captain Jacquard said. "And Rupert and Blake will go. For back up. But it's up to you to finish him."

"I'll go alone."

"No, you can't—"

She jerked her gaze to the captain. "If you want my help, you do it my way. I go alone or not at all."

She wasn't sure why she was so set on this suicidal course, but it just felt like something between her and Eli. And only them.

What kind of masochistic fool was she?

Chapter 14

With a heart weighted in sadness, Liberty drove to Eli's house. A dim light burned in his living room window. She climbed from the car and crept to the front door. Edging her way to the window, she tried to look inside the house, but the curtains were drawn and she couldn't see anything.

She recalled the last time she'd been in this very spot. That time she had been able to see. Eli feeding on a woman. The night she'd learned of the existence of vampires. But he hadn't been hurting her. It had been an... intimate thing. She shuddered. What he was doing lately was far removed from that. Nausea threatened to choke her. She took a deep breath through her mouth.

No choice but to go in. If the door was locked, she'd shoot it down. Then she'd shoot Eli. Did he have a girl with him right now? The thought made her blood freeze. If so, she had to move. Now.

She tried the door, surprised when the knob turned in her hand. She pushed it open and stepped inside.

Almost like a replay of the night she'd seen him with the other woman... he stood with his back to Liberty, a girl in his clutches. Her eyes were open. Staring at Liberty.

"Eli!" Liberty called out, her voice breaking.

Eli's shoulders tightened. He slowly lifted his head and turned to face her. His fangs protruded, his eyes were red, and gray wrinkles marred the flesh on his face. A shudder trembled through her. In seconds, he was back to normal. He frowned and wiped the blood from his mouth.

Her head swam dizzily—blood… on his mouth, from where he'd been feeding…

"Liberty? What are you doing here?"

She swallowed back bile. "Get away from her, Eli."

The girl was in her early twenties, attractive, tall with auburn hair.

"Shoot him," she screamed at Liberty.

"What?" Eli whirled back to her. "Why? We were having such a good time."

"He was trying to kill me," the girl sobbed.

Eli chuckled. "Kill you?" He looked back at Liberty. "She picked me up at Steamy Nights. Insisted I take her home. Offered herself to—"

"Shut up!" Liberty was disgusted with him, but at the same time, a part of her wanted to believe him. She pulled the gun from her waistband and pointed it at him. "Hands in the air."

He stared at her intently, his gaze flicking to the gun then back to her. "What's this all about?"

"I know."

"Know what?"

Tears threatened but she swallowed them back. "I know it's you. You're the vampire who murdered those girls."

Eli shook his head and chuckled. "Are you out of your mind?"

Liberty flicked a glance to the girl, keeping her attention on Eli. "Are you okay?"

Tears flowed from her eyes. She nodded. "Thank

God you got here, he would have killed me."

"What the hell? You're both crazy." Eli stepped toward Liberty.

"Stay where you are," Liberty ordered. "And hands up, now!" She wasn't sure how to take someone into custody, but she'd seen enough movies to know that having them raise their hands was a must. She wasn't really supposed to take him into custody, though. She was supposed to end his life.

"Liberty, what the hell is going on?"

"Give it up, Eli. The last girl survived. She ID'd you. And I know about the tree. It was you."

"Shoot him!" the girl screamed.

Eli didn't take his eyes off Liberty. "What about the tree?"

"The tree in the drawings. It was a Charter Oak. The tree that was outside your prison cell in Connecticut." Why was she explaining instead of pulling the trigger? Because, in spite of what he'd done, she didn't know if she could shoot him. Maybe she should let the authorities handle him. But she was supposed to take him out—end the line.

"How did you know about prison?"

"It doesn't matter, I know. I'm supposed to kill you but… I don't think I can." She pulled her phone from her pocket. The numbers swam through the tears blurring her vision. She dialed.

"Liberty…" He stepped closer.

"Don't move, or I will shoot."

"Kill him," the girl sobbed. "He was going to—"

"It's okay," Liberty interrupted. "You're going to be okay. Help will be here soon."

He lifted his hands in the air but took a step closer

to her. "I don't want to die with you thinking I'm guilty."

Liberty snorted a laugh. "Of course you're guilty. She just said you tried to kill her."

"I don't have an explanation for that. Not at the moment, but I know there is one. I swear on everything, I did not do this. I did not murder those girls. I need you to believe me."

She studied his eyes, those hypnotizing silver eyes, and saw… sincerity. She saw truth. But did she see that because she wanted to? "You told me once that I should never trust you."

He gave his charming lopsided grin. "I stand by that. But trust yourself. Search your heart. Do you really think I killed those girls?"

Moments stretched by with only the sound of the girl's sobbing. Finally, Liberty dropped the gun to her side and shook her head. "No, I don't believe you killed them."

"He's lying," the girl shrieked. "Can't you see that? Shoot him!" She lunged toward Liberty, reaching for the gun.

Reflexively, Liberty struck out to deflect the attack, and the gun caught the girl on the chin. She dropped heavily to the floor.

"Oh my God!" Liberty knelt to check her pulse. Eli squatted next to her and did the same.

"She's alive," he said. "Just unconscious."

Liberty covered her face with her hands. "I did this to her. I hurt her."

Eli took hold of Liberty's wrists and gently moved them away. "Listen to me, she's fine. She was obviously mesmerized. There's no telling what she might have done."

Liberty nodded and looked into his face. The confidence in his eyes fortified her, as did his touch.

She stood, and he released her. "We need to get out of here. They'll be here soon. I'm sure they expected to hear from me by now."

"I'm not running." Eli rose to his feet.

She frowned. "Not running? If you stay here, they'll kill you."

He smiled. "No, they'll make you do it."

"This isn't funny. Either way, you're dead if you stay. So let's go."

"I told you, I'm not running."

She brushed her hair back from her face. "We don't have much time." She stared at him, lifting her chin. "You can't mesmerize me and bend me to your will. If you don't come with me, I will tell them that I was a part of it. That we were working together."

"They'll never believe that. And if they do, they'll throw you in jail—or kill you too."

She shrugged. "I guess that's a chance I'm willing to take. If you won't go, then I'll go down with you."

He crossed his arms and narrowed his eyes. "What makes you think I care what happens to you?"

She met his gaze. "I suppose I'm about to find out."

He dropped his arms. "Damn stubborn female."

She smiled. "Come on." Liberty cast one more glance at the unconscious girl. "Are you sure she'll be okay?"

"Positive." He grinned. "You know, you are a bit of a bad ass."

In spite of the circumstances, she felt... light... happy. Insane. "So, where to?" she asked.

"You mean you don't have a plan?"

"I don't know this island like you do. Surely you have some idea where we can go."

"Yeah. I know a place." He grabbed a knapsack and shoved some items inside. "Let's go. But I'm warning you, I won't hide forever."

"You won't have to, just until we figure out what's going on."

"Yeah, at the rate we're going, that could be a couple of centuries. I have the time, but I don't think you do."

****

Liberty climbed into the passenger seat of Eli's car. Once they were underway, she said, "Where are we going?"

"To a friend's house. We can stay there until we decide on our next move."

"What do you think the girl will tell them?"

Eli took his eyes off the road long enough to flash her a grin. "That you couldn't resist my charms and you rode off into the sunset with me."

Liberty laughed. "Like they'd buy that."

After a few minutes, they pulled into the drive of a white two story house, surrounded by trees.

"Who lives here?" Liberty asked.

"Grace. She'll put us up until we formulate a plan."

She didn't try to keep the annoyance out of her voice. "Isn't there somewhere else we can go?"

"I don't have a plan, not right off the top of my head. For now, you'll be safe here."

"*I'll* be safe? You're staying too, right?"

He put a hand on his chest. "Aw, you would miss me, wouldn't you?"

She scowled as they climbed from the car. "I just don't want to stay with your—*friend*—by myself. I don't think she likes me."

"Grace is… well, Grace." He said it with such affection; she suffered a pang of jealousy. Gritting her teeth and shoving the unwanted emotion away, she followed him onto the porch.

Eli knocked and in seconds, the door opened. Grace's face lit with delight. She wore form fitting beige pants and a shimmery green blouse that set off her red hair. She was breathtaking, dammit. Liberty pursed her lips.

"Well, I'll be, dahlin'. What are you'all doin' here?"

Eli gave her a run-down of the events since they'd become involved in the case.

"Oh my. Sounds like you've got yourselves into a heap of trouble." She chuckled and stepped back to let them in. "Why, you come right on in here. Make yourself at home." Her eyes went to Liberty. "You too, kitten."

Grace led them across a wood-floored foyer into a large living area. The rose chintz upholstery and antique furnishings oozed southern charm.

"It's rather late—for humans," Grace said to Liberty. "I can show you up to the guest room if you want to get some shut eye."

Liberty shook her head. "I'm not tired. We need to work out a plan. I don't have time to sleep."

Grace lifted her shoulders in a graceful shrug. "Suit yourself. I'll prepare some refreshments."

Liberty dropped down onto the over-stuffed sofa. "So, how does Grace have this place? She doesn't live on the island, right?"

"Only part time. One of her husbands left this house to her. She has half a dozen or so homes all over the world that she acquired the same way." There was a note of admiration in his voice.

Liberty snorted. "So, in other words, she marries and uses men for their money. What, does she drain the life from them once they've served their purpose?"

"First of all, Miss Cynic. Grace *always* marries for love. Secondly, she doesn't have to kill them. She simply outlives them." His eyes were alight with amusement.

Maybe it was her lack of sleep and the rough few weeks she'd had, but she didn't find it all that damn funny.

She blew out a breath. "Whatever. So… here we are. You have any ideas?"

Eli settled onto the sofa next to her. "We never followed up on the eye witness mentioning the pink handkerchief. Maybe I should try to find Blackwell again."

"No." She shook her head. "I'm sure it wasn't him. The witness said the man had blue eyes. Besides, you need to stay out of sight."

"You think we can stay here and hide and this thing will resolve itself?"

Liberty stood and stalked across the floor, squeezing the hair on top of her head in her fist. "I don't know what to think. What to do."

"Well, we need to do something—and quick. We weren't getting anywhere when we were out beating the streets, and we damn sure won't get anywhere hiding."

Grace came into the room at that moment with a tray. "Coffee?" she asked Liberty.

"Yes, please."

Grace poured into a delicate rose-patterned cup and handed it to Liberty. She looked at Eli. "I have some nice, warm A-Neg for us."

Liberty couldn't control a sound of disgust. "Did you just drain that from a… you have someone back there?"

Grace snickered. "Oh no, kitten. We sometimes take a little extra and store it for later use. A few seconds in the microwave and it's as if we're feeding straight from the vein."

"Oh God, I'm going to be sick." Liberty put a hand to her chest and took a deep breath through her mouth.

"I'll just have coffee, thanks," Eli said.

Grace lifted her brows, but didn't comment as she poured a cup for Eli. The dainty china looked incongruous in his masculine hand.

"I have an idea," Grace said after she'd served herself a glass of thick, red, liquid. She rolled the goblet between her long, pale fingers. "Maybe I can help. I'll do some checking around and you two can stay hidden here."

Eli took a drink of the coffee, scowling. "I don't like the idea of cowering in fear."

Grace rolled her eyes. "You are not cowering. You are laying low until we figure this thing out." She frowned and touched a finger to her lips. "This man obviously has a vendetta against you." She smiled. "Of course, that gives us a frighteningly long list of suspects." She lowered gracefully onto an easy chair. "Tell me what we know so far."

Liberty averted her eyes when Grace took a sip of the blood.

They told her about the encounter with the human feeding on his fiancée, their theory that the vampire was mesmerizing witnesses and his victims, and about the pink handkerchief, which was pretty much all they had.

"I know Paul, and there is no way he would do anything that vicious." She winked at Eli. "Now you and I, not long ago… that's another story." A wistful look entered her eyes, as if she were fondly recalling the days of mayhem and plundering. She blinked and took another sip of her vile beverage, then looked at Eli. "What about Rupert? Blake? They certainly have no compunction when it comes to violence."

"I thought about that," Eli said. "But they have more to lose than anyone. They don't want the island to gain a dangerous reputation. It would become a ghost town and the vampires—on both sides—would starve. Or we would have to move on. And you know how much Rupert enjoys his reign here on Sang Croc."

Grace nodded. "True. Does Paul have anything against you?"

"Actually," Liberty interjected. "He seems to respect Eli—a lot."

Eli lifted his brows, but didn't quiz her. "The pink handkerchief could be another ploy, like mesmerizing the witnesses. Just something to throw us off track."

"Maybe you should un-mesmerize the girlfriend of the victim Liberty found," Grace said. "Grill her until she breaks."

"I don't think that's necess—" Liberty began.

"Yeah, that might work," Eli interrupted.

"Want me to fetch her?" Grace smiled like nothing would please her more.

"She's probably not even on the island anymore." Liberty's stomach tightened with worry. She had no idea what this Demented Duo might inflict upon that poor girl.

"Well, I suppose there's only one way to find out."

Grace stood and set her glass on the tray. She slid a knowing gaze from Liberty to Eli, then back to Liberty. "I presume you two will manage to… occupy yourselves while I'm gone?"

Liberty's face heated, and Eli chuckled. "We'll do our best."

Chapter 15

After Grace left, Eli insisted Liberty lay down. "You won't be any good to anyone if you don't rest. You should grab the opportunity now, while nothing is going on. Grace said you could use the guest room upstairs."

She gave in, but instead of going upstairs, she stretched out on the sofa in the front room. She didn't want to be too far away from whatever might happen in the next few hours.

Liberty tried to sleep, but every time she started to relax, she thought back to Ryan—how cold his voice had been when he told her he felt nothing for her. She should have known better than to fall for someone so quickly. Hadn't she learned anything from the Cam disaster? Not only was she starting to fall for Ryan, he was her best friend on the island. Someone she thought she could count on. Now, she felt more alone than ever.

Tears squeezed between her closed lids and spilled down her cheeks. She groaned and brushed them away, snuffling back a sob. Ridiculous. A vampire was out there stalking innocent girls and she was laying here feeling sorry for herself.

"Liberty? Are you okay?"

She hadn't head Eli come into the room. She rolled over, quickly wiping her face. The last thing she needed was him mocking her pain.

"Yeah, sure. I'm fine," she muffled in the depths of

the sofa.

Eli took her arm and pulled her up. He cocked his head and studied her. "Have you been crying?"

"No," she said, turning away from him. "Just having trouble sleeping, that's all."

He hooked his fingers under her chin and tugged gently. "Look at me."

With a sigh, she complied.

He narrowed his eyes. "You have been crying. What's wrong?"

"It's nothing."

He settled on the sofa next to her, and she scrunched to the back to give him room.

"Come on. If you're upset about something, you should tell me. We need to work together to find this guy, and I need you to be focused. So tell me. Is it your mom? Ryan?"

She shrugged. "I feel funny talking about it with you."

"Come on, we're pals right?"

Her heart dipped in her chest. *Pal* wasn't exactly how she thought of Eli. But she wouldn't go there. "Sure, yeah. Pals."

"And we have time to kill. It might make you feel better."

She drew in a deep breath and let it out slowly. "Yes, it's Ryan."

"What about him?"

She twisted her hands in her lap, hesitating before answering. "Something… happened. With us. He—just a few days ago, he said he loved me. And now…"

"Now what?" Eli's voice was soft, coaxing.

"Now he says we're—over. He doesn't feel

anything for me." She swallowed back more building in her throat. She would *not* cry over Ryan again. Especially not in front of Eli. "I don't understand what happened. He's always treated me so... special, made me feel cherished. I've never felt that way before." She shook her head. "Dumb, right?"

He gave a small smile. "Yeah, all that sappy love stuff is pretty dumb."

"A lot of help you are," she muttered under her breath.

His mouth twisted in a sardonic grin. "I said I would listen, I didn't say I could help." He rested his hand over hers. "But I am sorry."

"Thanks. I'll be fine." Silence fell between them. She gave a nervous laugh and slipped her hand from beneath his. "I guess we'd better get to work... doing something. Grace isn't back yet, is she?"

He stood and shook his head. "No."

She swung her legs over the side of the sofa and rose. "Is there any more of that coffee?"

"Half a pot or so."

She walked over and poured a cup. It was tepid, but it would do. "Grace has been gone a while. Are you worried about her?"

He laughed. "Grace can take care of herself."

"And if she gets in trouble, she can turn into a bat and fly away, right? How does that work exactly? If vampires can turn into bats so easily, why don't they do that every time they're threatened?"

"It doesn't quite work that way. We can't turn into a bat that easily. The reverse is the easy part—morphing from a bat back into vampire. In order to transform, you have to totally clear your mind, your emotions. It's an

135

instinct thing, which comes much easier in Chiroptera—that's the scientific name for bat—form."

"That makes no sense."

"When you think about it, it does. A bat's thought process is almost nonexistent so instinct takes over, and they just… morph. When we're in vampire form, it's harder to let go and allow the change to happen. A developed brain will overthink." He tossed out a wry smile. "Almost like our 'human' side. We won't rely as much on instinct and it's hard to focus enough, especially when your adrenaline is pumping, you're angry, scared, whatever."

"From what I've seen of Trey, his brain isn't much more developed than a bat. He can probably easily go either way."

Eli laughed. "Yeah, probably so. Why did you bring him up?"

"I had another confrontation with him."

Eli's expression darkened. "Did he hurt you?"

"No, but he hurt Hannah. He's… crazy. I keep wondering if he could be the one we're looking for. Whoever this person is, they don't seem to care about either vampire camp—or human life. That fits Trey perfectly."

"Why would he want to set me up?"

"I don't know. He wants me. Maybe he thinks you're in the way." She lifted her chin and looked into his eyes. "Are you?"

He gave a casual shrug. "I have no say in what happens to you. I'm neutral."

She snorted a bitter laugh. "Yeah, neutral toward me. That seems to be an epidemic."

"That's not what I—I'm sorry. I didn't mean—"

"No, don't. Just forget it. That makes me sound pathetic."

He seemed about to say more when his cell rang. He fished it from his pocket, looked at the display, and answered. "Hi Grace, I'm going to put you on speaker."

He pressed a button and Liberty heard Grace. "I didn't have any luck. The Skyler girl left the island, as did Paul. It appears he took off the day after he ran into Liberty."

"So he can't be our guy," Eli said.

"Right. Which we had already decided anyway. I haven't been able to—"

A small exploding sound came over the speaker, followed by a female cry.

Eli's face blanched. "Grace! Grace, are you okay?"

A moan, then a man's voice. "Grace, hey, is that you? What happened?"

"Blake," Eli said to Liberty. Into the speaker, he said, "Blake? Pick up the phone."

A fumbling sound, then Blake's voice. "Eli?"

"Yeah, is Grace okay?"

"She's been shot. But she's going to be okay. I have her now. She's safe."

A muscle ticked in Eli's jaw. "Who shot her?"

"I don't know. I don't see anyone around, but I'm getting her out of here in case they're still lurking."

"Are you sure she's okay?"

"I'm sure. I'm taking her to her house. She just needs time to heal. Where the hell are you, man? They're coming after you."

Liberty shook her head and mouthed, "Don't tell him. We'll get out of here."

Eli looked at her and said into the phone, "I'm at

Grace's. I'll be waiting for you to bring her. And hurry."

"Yeah, sure. But you know what I gotta do when I get there." A sound like footsteps, then a car door opening and closing, came over the speaker. "I'm sure Liberty's there. I don't know how you convinced her to take off with you, but you gotta turn yourself in."

"We can talk about that when you get here."

Eli tapped End on the cell and scraped a hand through his hair. Worry had darkened his eyes to slate grey.

"You can't stay here," Liberty said. "He'll kill you. Or take you in."

"I'm not leaving. Grace is hurt."

"He said she was fine." Hysteria made her voice shrill. "Eli, you have to get out of here. I'll wait and make sure Grace is okay, but you have to leave."

He gripped her upper arms and looked down into her face. "I didn't want to run the first time. I'm damn sure not running now and leaving her—or you—behind."

Tears choked her throat, and she jerked away. "Then congratulations, you're about to die." She crossed her arms and stalked away from him.

"Liberty, listen to me—"

She whirled to him. "No! I won't listen to another word. I risked my ass to keep you safe, now you're throwing it all away. We're both going down."

"I won't let them hurt you."

She gave a laugh that felt like a sob. "What the hell do you think you can do about it? You'll be dead."

He shut his eyes and shook his head. "I'm sorry. I can't go."

"Screw you, then. I can."

She strode to the door and flung it open, then halted,

gasping in surprise.

Blake stood on the porch, holding Grace in his arms. Her head lolled back and blood soaked her chest.

"Oh my God!" Liberty stepped back. "Is she okay?"

Blake's expression was grim. He brushed past Liberty and went into the living area, easing Grace down onto the sofa. "She will be. They missed her heart."

"Who's they?" Eli bit out.

Blake shook his head. "I have no idea. I didn't see anyone."

Grace's eyes fluttered. Her face was as white as bone. "Not—not my heart. Missed. I'll be fine, just need a-a minute." She drew in a labored breath. "But-he's... out there. He's coming."

"Who?" Eli squatted at her side. "Who's coming?"

She shook her head. "Didn't... see him." She panted between words. "Ambushed..."

"I'll find out who did this," Eli said gently, rubbing a thumb along her forehead. "I'll make them pay."

"Don't think so," Blake said. "You need to turn yourself in, man. You can't keep running." He looked at Liberty. "You helped him, didn't you? We wondered if you had, or if he'd forced you."

"We?" Liberty asked. "Are the police coming?"

Blake shook his head. "I separated from them, hoping to find Eli and talk some sense into him." His mouth turned down at the corners. "The police won't be in the mood to *talk* when they find him."

"He's innocent," Liberty said. "We're just trying to buy some time until we can prove it."

Blake chuckled. "Come on, you really believe that? How can you, with all the evidence?"

"Someone's setting me up." Eli said. "I don't know

who, but they're trying to pin this on me. I didn't do it."

"Eli, be realistic here. Who would want to frame you?"

"That's what I'm trying to find out," Eli snapped.

Blake narrowed his eyes. "I don't believe it. Let me take you in and you can stand trial."

"Trial?" Eli crooked a sardonic grin. "What happened to the order to take me out on sight?"

"I'll fix it," Blake said. "We'll give you a fair shake, but you have to come in. You don't have a choice. If you resist, not only will you be in danger, Liberty will too. They'll punish her right alongside you."

Eli's shoulders slumped. "Fine. I'll go in with you. But not until Grace is recovered."

Blake nodded. "Fair enough." He looked at Liberty. "You'll have some questions to answer too."

She glared at Eli and brushed angrily at the tears on her face. Why did she give a damn what happened to Eli? He had a chance to get away, and he hadn't taken it.

"She had nothing to do with this," Eli said to Blake.

Blake harrumphed. "She was supposed to bring you in. Instead, she fled with you. I doubt they'll take that lightly."

"She didn't come willingly. I forced her."

Blake narrowed his eyes and looked from Eli to Liberty. "Is that true?"

"It's true," Eli said before she could answer.

Liberty compressed her lips and didn't speak. She was tempted to deny it, to admit her part in Eli's escape, but if she wanted to find the culprit before something happened to Eli, she needed to remain free.

She bent over Grace and eased the edges of her blouse apart. A pink square of material lay on her chest just above her cleavage. Liberty gasped. A pink handkerchief? She glanced at Eli and saw that he'd noticed too.

"You stopped the bleeding?" Eli asked Blake casually.

"I did. She'll heal soon, but I didn't want her losing any more blood."

"So this is yours?" Eli lifted the handkerchief from Grace's wound.

"Yeah." Blake chuckled. "Not very manly, right?"

"Where did you get it?"

Blake frowned. "Why are you so interested?"

Eli shrugged. "It's just sort of unusual... for a man. And looks pretty expensive."

"Yeah, and familiar," Liberty said. "I ran into Paul Blackwell. He had a handkerchief just like this."

"Oh right. Blackwell is the one who told me about them. They come from an exclusive boutique in Switzerland. They're a special blend of Swiss Cotton and Linen. They only come in pink... so... well, you know. I got the pink."

"I didn't know you and Paul were tight," Eli said.

"We're not. We were both on holiday in Switzerland. I admired his handkerchief..." He scowled. "What's with the third degree?"

Liberty met Eli's eyes. She read his expression. He'd realized the same thing she had. It was Blake. The vampire they'd been after all this time was Blake.

Liberty eased her hand to the small of her back, reaching for her gun. The air around them shifted. Before Liberty's fingers touched the weapon, Blake snatched her by the hair and yanked her against his chest. Pain exploded in her head.

"Not so fast, little hunter." His maniacal laugh sent fear slithering up her spine. "I see the jig is up. Ah well, it was fun while it lasted. Now, someone's got to die."

Chapter 16

Eli shot to his feet and took a step toward Blake.

"I wouldn't do that." Blake's voice rumbled against Liberty's ear. "Not if you care what happens to her."

"Don't listen to him," Liberty choked out. Rage and pain vied for equal time in her heart. "He can't kill me."

Blake chuckled. Something sharp pressed against her neck. From the corner of her eye, she saw a knife.

"I can't kill you, but I can make you beg for death," Blake said.

Liberty squeezed her eyes shut, trying to summon courage. How much pain could she take? She wasn't sure, but she was willing to find out to end this asshole.

She opened her eyes and looked at Eli. "Take him out, Eli. Don't worry about me."

Eli's jaw tightened, his eyes glinting with rage. "I can't risk it."

Blake laughed. "I didn't think so."

Behind Eli, Grace sluggishly rose to a sitting position.

"Don't even think about it," Blake told her. "I shot you once. Don't think I won't do it again."

Eli's eyes narrowed. "So that was you?"

"Yeah. It was all me. I knew Grace had to be the one hiding you. I thought riding in like a hero would earn me your trust. It almost worked." He shook his head. "Who knew a handkerchief would be my tell?"

"Why?" Eli asked. "Why kill those girls and screw things up for your side?"

Blake shrugged. "I knew it would be nothing more than a temporary setback. And the long range payoff would be worth it."

"Long range payoff?"

"To destroy you." He eased his hold on Liberty's neck and wrapped an arm around her rib cage, holding her tightly against him. "I was really hoping your little girlfriend would take care of you for me, but I see you charmed her, just like you charm everyone else you come in contact with."

"Is that why you hate me?" Eli flashed a grin that didn't meet his eyes. "Jealous because of my charm?"

Blake's arm tightened, making it hard for Liberty to breathe. "I framed you because it's time someone brought to your knees. You need to learn, you can't be a golden boy in both worlds. You've had things your way your entire life. No more."

Eli shook his head. "That's not how it is."

"Oh, but that's exactly how it is. Even after your major betrayal, you're still Father's favorite. Now, though, he has to turn to me. His son who solved the murders."

Liberty's heart stuttered as Blake's words registered. She turned widened eyes to Eli. "Rupert is your father?"

Eli didn't answer. His focus was on Blake. "But if you'd had Liberty kill me, you wouldn't have been able to procreate, neither would Father. Our line would eventually die out."

"That's a risk I was willing to take. Now I don't have to worry about it. I can haul you in and you'll be executed, Father and I will be free to reproduce. As a bonus, I'll hold onto the Van Helsing bitch until the next full moon—then she's toast. And, voilà! No more hunting. Our numbers will increase like crazy."

Eli grunted a chuckle. "How do you think you'll capture all three of us? Grace is regaining her strength. Liberty is a hunter, and I'm, well…" His lips curled into a lethal smile. "…me."

Blake sniggered. "Never fear. I have a little something extra in my arsenal." He walked backwards, dragging Liberty with him, and headed toward the door, still keeping an eye on Grace and Eli.

Liberty looked for an opening, some kind of split second opportunity to make her move and take Blake out. But his grip was tight, and the knife never wavered from her neck. Even though he couldn't kill her, if he slit her throat, she wouldn't be much good to anyone until she healed.

When they reached the door, Blake moved the knife from Liberty's throat long enough to turn the knob. She used that moment to lift her feet off the ground. Although Blake was inhumanly strong, he'd relaxed his hold, and the sudden shift was enough to throw him off balance. He released her, and she dropped to the ground.

She scrambled to her feet and whirled to confront Blake, but he was already out the door.

"Shit," she muttered.

Eli rushed into the foyer, Grace behind him, and put a hand beneath Liberty's chin, lifting her gaze to his. "Are you okay?" His eyes searched her face, and worry etched his features.

She nodded. "I'm fine, but I let him get away." She withdrew from Eli's touch and yanked open the door.

Her gaze searched the yard. Thick trees rustled in the light wind, and Grace's outside lights illuminated the area. A Lexus sat next to Eli's Corvette but there was no sign of Blake. "Where did he go?" Liberty muttered. She glanced back at Eli. "What do you think he has in his arsenal?"

"I don't know, but you need to get back," Eli said. "I'm not sure what he meant, but one thing he has is a gun. Until we know where he is, you need to stay out of—"

A gunshot sounded and the door next to Liberty's ear splintered. Eli grabbed her and dove to the floor, sheltering her body with his. "—sight," he finished with a wry grin.

Liberty let out a breath, her heart beating a thousand beats per second.

"Jesus. He's bat shit crazy—no pun intended," Grace said.

Liberty crouched beneath the picture window that looked out over the yard. She eased upward until she could get a view of the outside.

"We can't just let him go," she whispered.

"No," Eli said. "I'll go after him."

Liberty grabbed his arm. "Then he'll shoot *you*."

Eli shrugged. "Maybe, but we're running out of options."

Liberty bit her lip. "He can't have gone far. He wants to silence the three of us, so he'll show himself."

"Smart girl." Blake's voice came from a cluster of trees at the back of the yard. "I'm not leaving until I get what I want."

"I don't think you're in a position to bargain," Eli said. "It's over. You might as well give up."

"Ah, but you're forgetting about the added insurance, brother."

Eli chuckled. "You're bluffing. You've got nothing. You're just humiliated because Liberty managed to thwart you. Does that make you feel a little foolish, *brother*?"

For several moments there was no movement, then a flash bolted from the trees to the rear of the Lexus. Blake opened the trunk, obscured from view for a split second. The trunk closed, and Blake held a girl in front of his body. A young, blonde girl.

Liberty's heart dipped to her stomach. "Oh my God." She brought a hand to her mouth to hold back a cry. "He's got Hannah."

The girl trembled in his grasp. Even from this distance, Liberty could see tears pouring down her cheeks.

"Liberty?" Hannah wailed. "Help me. Please… help me."

Blake clamped a hand over the girl's mouth. "You have exactly five seconds to surrender—the three of you—or I'll rip her head off."

"Go ahead," Eli said. "Why should I care?"

Liberty whirled to him. "Are you out of your mind?"

"Yeah, that's what I thought." Blake moved a step closer to the house. "You're willing to risk it, but I don't think your girlfriend is."

Liberty shouted to Blake, "Don't hurt her. I'll come out, but please don't hurt her."

"You're not going anywhere," Eli gritted. "We just need to stall."

"While we're stalling, Hannah might die."

Grace whispered, "I'm going to work my way

around the back and try to get the jump on him."

"You'll get Hannah killed," Liberty said quietly. She looked at Eli. "We can't let her die."

"Trust me, sugah," Grace purred. "I know what I'm doing. Keep him occupied."

Grace zipped away toward the back of the house.

Liberty's stomach clenched, and she blinked back tears. "He's going to kill her."

"No, he's not," Eli said.

"You don't know that."

"He wants me. I'll go out there, and maybe Grace and I together can get Hannah out of harm's way. You stay here."

"But he'll kill you."

"You have no faith in me at all, do you?" He winked. "I'm invincible." He planted a quick kiss on her lips that was over before she realized what had happened. Even in the middle of a crisis, disappointment shot through her. "In case this goes badly," he said. "I need to tell you something."

Hope bloomed in her chest. Eli was finally going to tell her how he felt. It was likely too late, but at least she would know. Once and for all.

"Ryan still loves you."

She blinked. It took a few moments for his words to sink in. "What? How do you know?"

"Because. It's my fault he said he didn't."

"How is it your fault?"

"I mesmerized him to stop loving you."

"You what?"

"The night after your last date. I was waiting for him when he came home. And I... made him believe he had no feelings for you. I told him to be cold to you. I

148

mesmerized him."

"You—you what?" She didn't believe it. Couldn't believe it. "Why? Why would you do that?"

He shrugged. "Moment of insanity. The sappiness was making me ill."

"Bullshit." She gritted her teeth. "That was a horrible thing to do. You can come up with a better reason than that." She grabbed his arm. "Tell me the truth. Why did you do it?"

"What do you want to hear, Liberty? Some kind of declaration about how, even though I can't have you I don't want to see you with anyone else? Is that what you want me to say?"

Yes. She kept her voice low, steady. "What I want is honesty. For once, the truth from you, that's all I want."

He laughed and shook his head. "The truth is, I'm a son of a bitch. Period. I can't tell you why I did it, because I don't know. I just did. So let it go, Liberty."

She compressed her lips and didn't speak. Anger and hurt boiled inside her, but she put it out of her mind. Right now, her concern was for Hannah.

Eli stood, stepped to the front door, and called out to Blake, "Let her go."

Blake's chuckle filtered to Liberty. "Hmmm… I don't know. First, we'll see how she tastes."

Liberty shot to her feet and rushed past Eli, but he grabbed her arm and snatched her back.

"Let go," she gritted. He didn't budge. She leveled him a poisonous look and shouted to Blake, "Don't hurt her… please. I'll do whatever—"

"Shut up, Liberty." Eli cut her off. "She's not worth it."

"Not worth it?" Anger choked her voice, and she

barely got the words out. She stared at him in disbelief. "Are you insane?" She jerked against Eli's hold and started toward Blake.

Eli tightened his grip and yanked her back to his side. "You're not going out there."

She struggled, but it was like trying to bend steel. "Let me go. I can't let him—devour that poor little girl. I hate you, Eli. Let me go!"

Blake's laughter rang out. "I'll make you a deal. I drink until you both surrender."

He bent his head to Hannah's neck. The girl's scream was almost drowned out by Liberty's. Movement in the yard caught Liberty's attention. Grace was heading toward Blake.

"Eli," Liberty ground out. "Let me go, or I'll never forgive you."

He gave a sardonic grin. "As much as you have to forgive me for, I doubt you'll ever forgive me anyway. I'll take my chances."

Tears flowed down Liberty's cheeks. She watched helplessly as Hannah's body went limp in Blake's grasp.

Get to her, Grace, please help her…

Grace lunged and at the same moment, Blake released Hannah and staggered back. He let out an agonized roar and gripped his hair, tugging and shrieking.

"What the…?" Shock froze Liberty's heart.

Blake's hands clawed his face, and blood spurted. Grace scooped Hannah up in her arms and stumbled back, her eyes glued to Blake.

"Hannah still has your blood in her system," Eli said, dropping his hands from Liberty.

"You—you knew that."

He tightened his jaw. "Yeah, I knew. Antoine told me about having to replenish your vials."

An agonized scream ripped through the night. Blake fell to the ground and plunged the knife into his chest, over and over, each stab punctuated by screams of agony.

"Oh my God," Liberty choked out. She yanked her gun from its holster and ran out the door and across the yard, aiming at Blake.

She narrowed her eyes on his heart—focused on her target—squeezed the trigger. Blake's body jerked, then he went still. In seconds, his body bubbled and flamed, then sizzled to a pile of ash.

Eli appeared at her side. "Why didn't you let him suffer?" His voice was cold, but the sheen in his eyes conveyed his emotion.

"I… just… couldn't."

Eli nodded. He stood over his brother's remains, not speaking.

Liberty rushed to Hannah's side. Grace had lowered her to the soft grass and was kneeling beside her. Hannah's eyes were shut, but her chest rose and fell. She was alive, thank God.

"She passed out," Grace said. "Which is probably a blessing under the circumstances."

"Yeah," Liberty whispered. "I'm not sure how many times we can make her forget what she's seen."

Grace gave a humorless smile. "As many times as it takes, sweetheart. As many times as it takes."

****

Once she finally arrived home, Liberty slept for twelve hours straight, surprisingly with no nightmares— or at least none she remembered. The police had questioned them at Grace's since the sun was coming up and Eli couldn't travel into town. The investigation was still ongoing, but with Hannah's account of Blake kidnapping her—the one thing about the night Eli hadn't made her forget—and with the fact that Blake had driven out to Grace's on his own and not called his father or the authorities, Captain Jacquard was leaning toward believing Liberty and Eli's account of what had happened.

She lay in bed, dreading getting up, dreading work, but since she was due for her shift at six—in less than an hour—she forced herself out of bed and into the shower.

Ryan was the first person she saw when she walked into the Getaway—probably because her eyes always zeroed in on where she expected him to be.

He spotted her and rounded the bar, hurrying over. "Liberty? Are you okay?" His dark eyes searched her face. "Oh my God. I thought I'd lost you."

"Lost me? You *dumped* me. And I'm fine, but why do you care?" In spite of what he'd done, her traitorous heart hoped he *did* care.

He let out a pained chuckle. "I deserve that. I'm so sorry for the way I treated you."

She shrugged. "It's no big deal." Odd that he remembered what he'd done while mesmerized. She hadn't known it worked that way, but then, she'd never seen anyone *de*-mesmerized. There was still a great deal to learn. "So much has happened I haven't even had time to digest it all."

"But I don't want to lose you. Please give me another chance."

Just because Eli had removed the mesmerization, it didn't mean she was going to fall back into Ryan's arms so easily. He'd hurt her—intentionally or not. That wasn't something she could just forget. She turned away from him and tied an apron around her waist. "Can we talk about this later?"

The front door opened, and Eli walked in, his long, lazy stride and silver eyes making her pulse rate speed up.

Without looking back at Ryan, she approached Eli.

"Hi." Was all she could manage.

"Hi back." His smile didn't help slow her racing heart.

"I'm sorry. About your brother. That must have been difficult."

Eli shrugged. "We weren't that close."

In spite of the nonchalant attitude, she saw deep pain in his eyes. "So how is it you and Rupert have different last names?"

"I took my mother's surname. I didn't want anything to do with Rupert once I left the EO's."

"I see." She drew in a breath. "I guess I should thank you. I mean, I'm still pissed that you mesmerized Ryan, but thank you for undoing it." She laughed dryly. "But then, I'm still not sure I can trust his feelings. How do I know what's real since you mesmerized him? Maybe he really stopped caring, but now you screwed with his head some more, and he thinks he loves me again."

"I didn't undo it."

"What? But, he said he loved me."

"Did he?" Eli looked over her shoulder to Ryan, then back at her. "Damn, that's some powerful love."

She frowned. "What do you mean?"

"Like I said, I didn't undo it. That's what I'm here to do now."

"Seriously?" She looked back at Ryan uncertainly. He was behind the bar again, watching them with narrowed eyes. "Wow," she breathed.

"Yeah, the dude must have it bad to overcome my powers of persuasion. Those are some deep feelings."

Liberty pursed her mouth, considering. "I still don't know that I can trust him, but if he loves me that much… maybe there's hope."

"I'd say he deserves a shot."

She looked into Eli's eyes. "Is that what you think I should do? Give him another shot?"

He studied her for a moment, then nodded. "That's exactly what I think you should do."

An odd feeling of something missed, disappointment combined with relief, coursed through her. "Okay then." She forced a smile. "We'll see how things go."

"Good idea. I'll catch you later."

"Yeah. Catch you later," Liberty whispered, not looking back at Eli. She headed to the bar. She wasn't ready to go all in with Ryan, but whatever might have been with Eli would never be. He'd made that painfully clear.

****

"I do declare, in all my born days I've never heard such a whopper of a lie."

Eli looked over his shoulder. Grace stood just inside the door of the Getaway.

He scowled. "Knock it off, *Scarlett*. You were listening?"

"I was outside when I heard all that foolishness." She shook her head. "But I know the truth. You *had* already undone the mesmerization. You lied to her and pushed her into his arms. What's wrong with you? This was your chance to swoop in."

"What's the point? We can never have a future together."

"Future, smuture." Grace snorted. "You could have had the fling of a lifetime with a girl you're crazy about. Then get her out of your system."

Eli barked a laugh and shook his head. He glanced toward the bar in time to witness Ryan brush a lock of hair from Liberty's forehead. The smile she gave the lucky bastard sent a pang through Eli's gut. He clenched his jaw and heaved a sigh. "'Fraid not. Liberty isn't the kind of girl you have a fling with—or someone you could ever get out of your system."

An Excerpt from *Liberty Empowered*, Book 3 in the Isle of Fangs Series…

Chapter 1

Sang Croc Island,
French Polynesia

Hannah Rankin just barely resisted the urge to stomp her foot. Her grandparents already treated her like a child, she couldn't give them any more reason to think of her that way. She was *fourteen years old*, for God's sake.

She crossed her arms tightly over her chest, but managed to keep her feet still. "Please, can't we stay? I don't want to leave Sang Croc."

"Honey, we've been here four months." Her grandmother folded one of Hannah's shirts with the ease born of years of practice and laid it gently in the open suitcase. She glanced at Hannah with a sympathetic smile. "You have to go back and start school."

"Let me go to school here."

"We can't live here. Our home is in Oklahoma." Her grandmother's brow creased. She wrung her hands together. Any kind of conflict made her nervous. Hannah usually didn't argue with her, but this was mega important.

Her grandfather spoke from where he sat on the hotel sofa. "Look, I know you'll miss Liberty. But you can keep in touch on the Facebooks."

His misuse of the word normally amused or annoyed her. Now, she was too worried for it to do either. Liberty wasn't the reason she wanted to stay. She liked her and would miss her, but the main reason she didn't want to leave was because of the Cave of Youth. Somewhere on this island was a cave that held magical water that restored youth. If she could find it, she could help her grandparents. They'd raised her after her piece of crap mother abandoned her. They were getting old, and she couldn't lose them. God, what would she do if she lost them? Go back to her drugged out mother?

Her throat clogged with tears and this time, she did stomp her foot. "If you make me go, I'll never speak to you again."

Her grandmother's mouth dropped open, and tears welled. Hannah looked away to prevent hurtling into in her arms and begging for forgiveness.

"You apologize right now, young lady." Her grandfather's voice was unusually harsh.

The apology was on the tip of her tongue, but she choked it back. She was *right*, dammit. "No, I will not!" She whirled and ran out of the room, slamming the hut door behind her.

She listened for the sounds of her grandparents following her. Even if they did, they were too old, they'd never catch her.

Her breath heaved in and out. A twinge of guilt surfaced. Her grandparents had been awesome. They loved her. Took care of her. Treated her great. So why was she being such a bitch?

Because… they just wouldn't *listen*. She was only trying to *help* them. Couldn't they see that?

Tears blinded her as she ran down the beach toward the ocean. Maybe she should just dive in and not come back up. She'd rather be dead than end up back with her mother—

A figure appeared from nowhere directly in front of her. She skidded to a halt, barely in time to keep from slamming into him. What the *F*? Her heart thudded. She panted, trying to catch her breath. He was tall—extremely tall—with shaggy dark hair that fell over his forehead and accentuated unusually pale skin.

"Uh, excuse me." She started around him, but he stepped in front of her. She peered up at him, her heart pounding even harder. "I'm sorry. If you could just let me by…" She tried to strengthen her voice, but between the tears, the running, and terror, she didn't succeed.

Something moved in her peripheral vision, and suddenly, there were two more guys with him. One was short and thin, with a goatee and spiked brown hair. The other was almost as tall as the first. His arms were covered in tattoos. They were equally pale-skinned.

"Ah." The first one gave a creepy smile. "Just who we were looking for."

"Looking for?" Her voice came out in a squeak. "Me?" She glanced behind her. Nothing but pure darkness. Would her grandparents come after her? She swallowed and backed away. "I'm sorry, I need to…"

With each step she took, the vampires took one as well, walking slowly toward her.

Panic thrummed through her body, making her knees tremble. She backed away more quickly, preparing to turn and flee, but afraid to take her eyes off them. "If you touch me, I'll scream. My grandparents will hear, and they'll come out."

The first guy chuckled. "Oh yeah, they'll definitely come out. We're counting on it." She barely saw him move, but in an instant, she was plastered against his chest, his arm around her waist, her feet dangling above the ground. She let out a yelp, shoving against him with all her might.

He didn't budge. He lifted an eyebrow, and a slow, chilling grin spread across his face. "So, where's that scream you promised?" He opened his mouth and showed his teeth... not normal teeth... fangs... A... vampire?

Her legs shook. Terror froze her flesh. "Please... oh please..." she whimpered. Her heart vibrated so hard she thought it would explode. He bent his head toward her neck. She let out a blood curdling scream.

****

One week later

An evening breeze blew in from the ocean, lifting and then lowering the target that hung between two coconut palm trees. Liberty Van Helsing drew in a deep breath and focused, repeating her new mantra, *the fewer vampires you kill, the more humans that die.* She *had* to improve as a hunter. Lives depended on it.

She shook out her shoulders, planted her feet in the sand, gripped the butt of the pistol, and narrowed her eyes on the target. She drew in a lungful of ocean air, and—

A hurtling object flashed in her peripheral just before something slammed into her shoulder. She stumbled, the gun went off—and she missed the target completely.

She lifted her upper body and rested on her elbows. "Son of a bitch!" A Frisbee lay on the beach a few feet away. She sprang to her feet, brushing sand off her jeans and whirled on Eli, who leaned nonchalantly against a palm tree. "What the hell?"

He grinned. "A little distraction."

"You threw a *Frisbee* at me? While I was taking aim?"

"Do you think the EO's will wait for you to settle into your stance on a hunt?"

She huffed out a breath. "Maybe not, but you could have given me a head's up."

He pushed off the tree and sauntered toward her, stopping a few inches away, his dark blond hair blowing in the wind like a tarnished halo.

Her breathing slowed, the way it did every time he came near. She squelched the urge to back away. Forcing herself to meet his glittering silver gaze, she lifted her chin.

He tightened his jaw and gritted out, "The Evil Ones aren't going to give you a head's up, Liberty. They're going to come at you, as fast and hard as they can. You have to be ready, for anything. Especially now that Rupert has called off the truce."

She shrugged, doing her best to conceal how terrified she was that the enraged leader of the EO's had a vendetta against her. "Rupert will calm down. He'll give up."

He grunted a disbelieving laugh. "You don't know Rupert. He never gives up."

"Are you afraid of him?"

"I'm not afraid for me. He might make me suffer, but he'll never kill me." A muscle ticked in his jaw, and he looked out toward the water. "But he'll come after you. He'd like nothing more than to hurt someone I lo—" He jerked his gaze back to her with a grimace. "Someone I care about."

Love? Had he been about to say he *loved* her?

No, and even if he was, what did it matter? She didn't feel that way about him. She was a vampire hunter. She couldn't feel that way about a vampire.

"Speaking of Rupert…"

Eli edged back, eyes wary. "Yeah?"

"Aren't we going to talk about his being your father? About what happened between you two?"

"Nothing to talk about. He's my father, a fact I'd rather forget, end of story."

"How did you wind up defecting from the Evil Ones?"

"It's a long story."

"We have plenty of time."

"No, we don't. We need to use our time wisely, so we don't have to send you back to Oklahoma in a body bag."

"A body bag?"

"Yeah, you know, because you're such a lousy shot."

Her hackles rose. "I'm not a lousy shot."

"You had, what, half a dozen chances at Trey, and still missed his heart?"

Her shoulders fell. He was right. Trey was an unstable, vicious vampire and she'd barely escaped his attacks more than once. She might have learned a lot since coming to Sang Croc from Oklahoma—how to shoot a bow, how to fight—but she couldn't hit the broad side of a hut with her gun. She let out an exasperated breath. "Face it, I'll never be the hunter my father was."

"No, you won't. But you don't have to be a complete failure. The full moon is a week away. You have to be ready by then."

She crossed her arms over her chest and frowned.

"It's my birthday," she blurted, then immediately wished she could take it back.

"What's your birthday?"

She dropped her arms, exasperated with herself for sounding like a petulant child. "On the full moon night, next Sunday. It's my nineteenth birthday." And the first one she'd spend without her mother. She hadn't seen her in four months. It seemed like a lifetime. An ache filled her chest, and she drew in a shuddering breath. She missed her so much.

"So."

Liberty lifted her brows. "*So*?"

He shrugged. "It's just a birthday. If you don't want it to be your last, we better get back to training."

Asshole. She tightened her lips and glanced down the beach where the unharmed target hung, silhouetted by the golden pink dusk that hovered above the water.

"Maybe Ryan will care, even if you don't."

He chuckled. "Are you trying to make me jealous?"

Was she? She hoped not. She didn't want to be *that* girl. Besides, she and Ryan weren't even together, at least not like a couple. But Ryan was so much more *caring* than Eli.

"No, I'm not trying to make you jealous. Just pointing out that Ryan is much nicer to me than you are."

"Nice never stopped a raging group of vampires." He picked the gun up and thrust it toward her. "Now, shoot."

She snatched it from his hand, whirled to the target, lifted the gun, and squeezed the trigger. A hole blasted through the silhouette, just to the left of center. Excitement zipped through her, and she turned back to Eli with a smile. "I did it! That was good, right?"

He grinned. "Yeah, that was good." He took her shoulders and twisted her body to face the target. "Now, do it again."

Two hours later, after she'd practiced until she thought her arms would fall off, she began to see improvement. She wasn't where she needed to be, but if she practiced every night until the hunt, maybe she would survive.

"Okay, now for the last part of your lesson." Eli took hold of her shoulders and gently kneaded them. As always, she marveled at how his cool vampire flesh could incite a heated rush through her veins with one little touch. She pushed back those thoughts. Eli was off limits for many reasons. Not only was he a vampire and she a hunter, he was unpredictable, always seemed on the verge of doing something rash, something with fatal consequences. Besides, he'd made it clear they could never be together. It was her duty to carry on the Van Helsing name, and she couldn't do that if she hooked up with a vampire.

"What are we doing?" She could barely manage a choked whisper over the lump in her throat. Damn… why did his nearness make her insides quiver?

"If you want to be a successful hunter, you'll have to tap into the speed and strength of the Van Helsing lineage."

"I keep hearing that, but I don't know how."

"I'm going to help. Close your eyes."

Her eyes drifted shut. A small shudder quivered through her.

"Feel the blood coursing through your veins." Deep, husky tones washed over her skin. "In your blood, there is power."

"But I don't know how to—"

"Shhh, don't talk. Just feel."

She took a slow deep breath of salty air. In the distance, ocean waves lapped on the shore and sea gulls squawked. Eli was so near, she could hear his heart beating. How did he expect her to focus when he was so… close? She swallowed loudly, pushing aside thoughts of Eli.

Focus…

Concentrating on the blood rushing through her veins, she made the effort to feel instead of think. The energy. The power. In that blood was the Van Helsing gene. Her father and his father before him, all had the power, the speed and strength of the Van Helsings. She may not have known her father long, but she was still his child… a Van Helsing.

Strong, fast, a hunter…

Nothing. Not a hint of the elusive Van Helsing power. She grunted in frustration and opened her eyes. "I can't do it."

Eli gripped her arms. "You *can.* You're a Van Helsing."

"Yeah, well I only found that out four months ago, and so far, I don't *feel* like a Van Helsing."

"You've been on three successful hunts."

"Yes. I killed a few vampires. Fortunately, I only ran into a few. What is going to happen when I'm face to face with a group of them? I'm toast, that's what."

"If you think you are, then you are."

She twisted away from him and let out an irritated sigh. "Thanks for that bit of insight, oh wise one."

He gave a small mock bow. "Any time."

"Listen, I'm going to call it a night." She brushed

wayward strands of hair back from her face. "This is useless."

He shook his head. "If you give up that easily, you'll never become the hunter you need to be."

"I could practice twenty-four/seven for the rest of my life, and I still will never be the hunter I need to be."

He growled and opened his mouth to speak, then snapped it shut and whirled toward the tree line. Liberty followed his gaze. She didn't hear anything, didn't see—

A figure burst from the trees, running straight for them. Liberty lunged for her gun, one knee in the sand. She took aim, finger tensed on the trigger. A few yards away, a young girl swayed, eyes wild and darting from side to side. Her blood-soaked blouse hung in tatters on her thin frame.

A word about the author…

Alicia Dean began writing stories as a child. At age 10, she wrote her first ever romance (featuring a hero who looked just like Elvis Presley, and who shared the name of Elvis' character in the movie, Tickle Me), and she still has the tattered, pencil-written copy. Alicia is from Moore, Oklahoma and now lives in Edmond. She has three grown children and a huge network of supportive friends and family. She writes mostly contemporary suspense and paranormal, but has also written in other genres, including a few vintage historicals.

Other than reading and writing, her passions are Elvis Presley (she almost always works in a mention of him into her stories) and watching (and rewatching) her favorite televisions shows like Ozark, Dexter, Justified, Breaking Bad, Sons of Anarchy, and Vampire Diaries. Some of her favorite authors are Michael Connelly, Dennis Lehane, Stephen King, Lee Child, Lisa Gardner, Ridley Pearson, Joseph Finder, and Jonathan Kellerman…to name a few.

Email: Alicia@AliciaDean.com
Website: http://aliciadean.com/
Blog: http://aliciadean.com/alicias-blog/
Facebook:
https://www.facebook.com/AuthorAliciaDean/
Twitter: @Alicia_Dean_
Instagram: AliciaDeanAuthor

BookBub: https://www.bookbub.com/profile/alicia-dean

Pinterest: https://pinterest.com/aliciamdean/

Goodreads:
http://www.goodreads.com/author/show/468339.Alicia_Dean

www.ingramcontent.com/pod-product-compliance
Lightning Source LLC
Chambersburg PA
CBHW070548180626
46817CB00005B/1739